Crystal Saga Series 3

7 – The Saga of Planet X . . . and Beyond

8 – What's Next?

D. E. Weingand

Crystal Saga Series 3

7 – The Saga of Planet X . . . and Beyond
8 – What's Next

A Crystal Saga Series

ISBN: 979-8-218-29224-9

Published by D. E. Weingand, Florence, Oregon 97439.

Printed in the United States of America.

Front cover photo by D. E. Weingand. Design by Luanna K. Leisure.

Luanna K. Leisure, Little White Feather Graphic Designer, and Independent Publisher. Campbell, California.

To order additional books go to: **http://www.LuLu.com, Amazon.com or Barnesandnoble.com**
Email: weingand@me.com

The Saga of Planet X . . . and Beyond
Crystal Saga Series 3
Book 7

Table of Contents

Book 7

Table of Contents Continued

What's Next?
Crystal Saga Series 3
Book 8

Table of Contents

AKURA

LIGHT SIDE

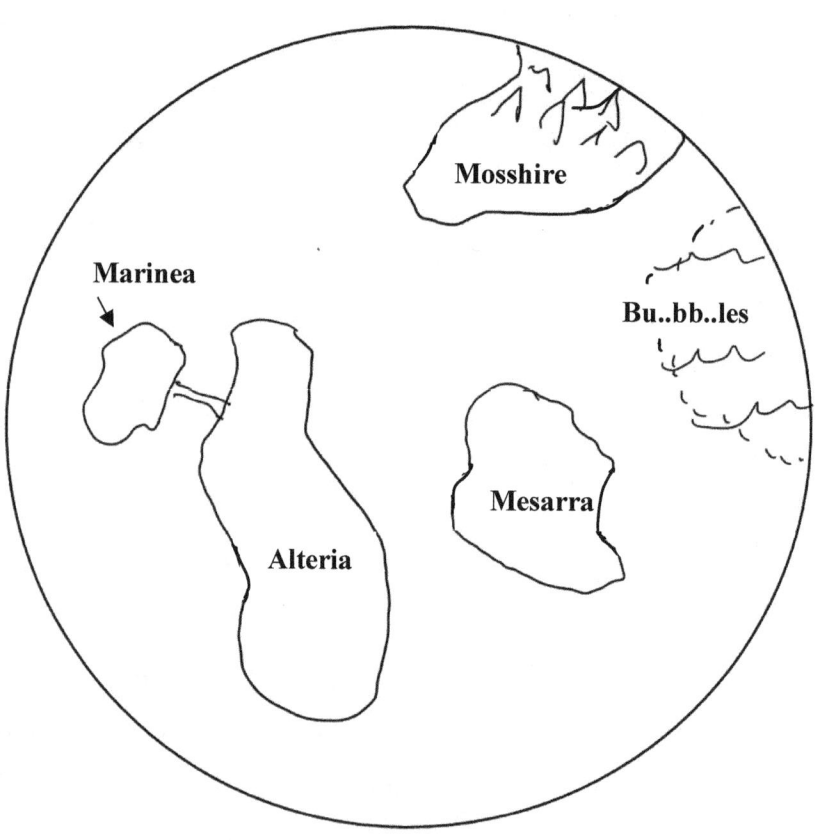

AKURA

DARK SIDE

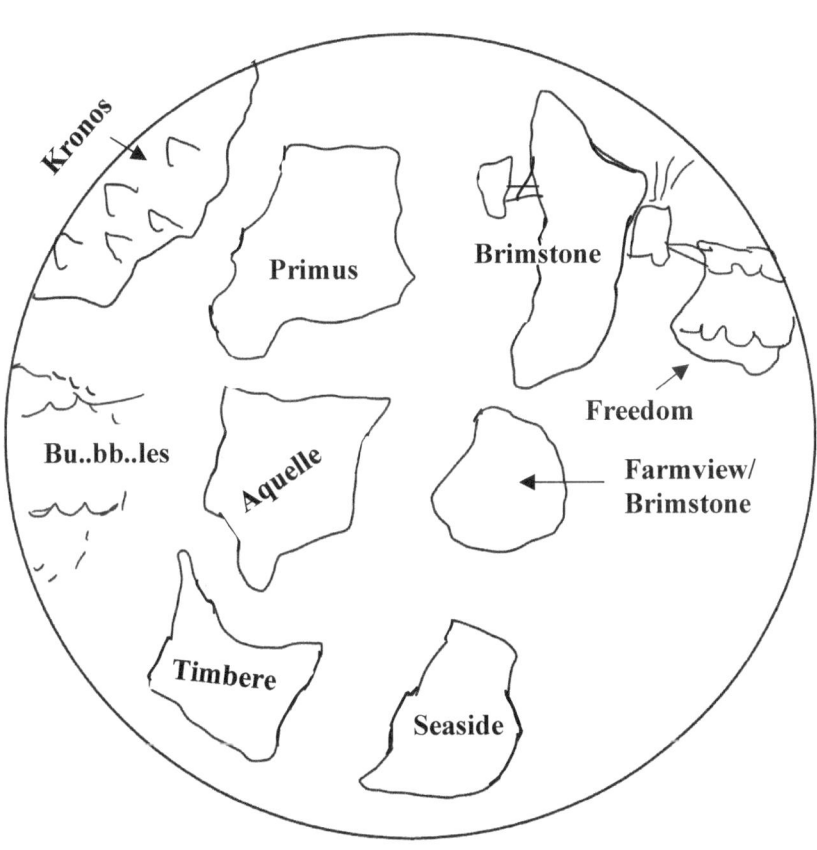

Setting and Geography

Akura...A planet

(On the light side of the planet)

Alteria...The land kingdom which succumbed to the Great Quakes. The remaining land portion is governed by a Council of Elders. Alterians have hazel eyes and blonde hair.

Marinea...The kingdom under the sea formed after the Great Quakes divided the land kingdom of Alteria. Marineans have silver hair and eyes and were governed by kings, now by Queen Tamara. They have retractable gills in order to live on both land and sea.

Mosshire...A land kingdom in the cold north composed of small pieces of forested, ice-covered land joined by bridges, and an impenetrable mountain range. Ruled by Sostor, an ice magic sorcerer. Residents have fair skin, blonde hair and very blue eyes.

Mesarra...A land kingdom in the south composed of a great desert. Residents are from tribes ruled by Sunan, a solar magic mage. Residents have very dark hair, skin and eyes.

*   *   *   *   *

(On the dark side of the planet)

Primus...A verdant kingdom with many greenhouses and well-designed buildings. Subject to seismic activity. Ruled by King Forty, the fortieth king in the sequence of rulers.

Aquelle...A kingdom that includes a huge lake that feeds into the ocean. There are many boats and bridges that offer connections to a series of islands. Previously ruled by King Scimitar; now governed through elections, currently by President Regis.

Timbere…A kingdom situated in a large forest with treehouses linked by aerial pathways. Ruled by Queen Flora III, a Super Sister and Twin to Queen Astrid.

*   *   *   *   *

Brimstone…A mountainous kingdom with many caves. Previously ruled by King Lucas, a wielder of shadow magic. Now ruled through election by Lucian.

Farmview…A kingdom supplying the kingdom of Brimstone, now part of Brimstone.

Freedom…An undersea kingdom populated by refugees from Brimstone; ruled by Cyril and his twin brother, Cyrus, both identified as Super Children/Twins.

Seaside…A kingdom on the sea. Ruled by Queen Astrid, a Super Sister and Twin of Queen Flora III.

*   *   *   *   *

Kronos…A kingdom beneath the mountain range behind Mosshire. Ruled by King Rupert II, a Super Brother and Twin of Shamous from the kingdom of Marinea. Residents are Elves.

'Bu..bb..les'…A kingdom beneath the 'endless sea' between Kronos and Marinea. Part of both light and dark sides of Akura. Ruled by King Posidon; residents are mermaids and mermen.

*   *   *   *   *

On another astral plane…

<u>The Crystal Castle</u>

Home of the Super Beings and their Watcher/Guardians.

Elsewhere in the Universe. . .

Starbright...a planet

Starlight... An alien kingdom recently ruled by a King and Queen, killed in a crash of their airship on Akura. Now succeeded by their daughter, Trixie, a Super Child living on the planet Akura.

Starshine... An alien kingdom originally ruled by Queen Bella, who had been imprisoned by the leaders of a military uprising.

*   *   *   *   *

Planet X...a planet

A planet responsible for the unsolved kidnapping of Queen Tamara and Queen-Designate Candace of Marinea. Now threatened by its star going Super Nova.

Bluegreen...a planet

Planet #1 in the search for a new home suitable for the residents of Planet X.

Cloudy...a planet

Planet #2 in the search for a new home suitable for the residents of Planet X.

Robotic...a planet

Planet #3 in the search for a new home suitable for the residents of Planet X.

Winner...a planet

Planet #4 in the search for a new home suitable for the residents of Planet X.

Cast of Characters (Arranged by Kingdom)

(On the light side of Akura)

<u>Marinea</u>

Tamara…Queen of Marinea; a Super Child and Sister/Twin to Trina. Married to Sean.

Sean…Commander of the Marinean Security Force, Tamara's husband, and a Super Child/Twin to Jon.

Candace (Candy), Sunny, Skye and **Verd**…Children of Tamara and Sean. Original Super Children with no mirror twins.

Leilani and **Andrea**…The new Super Children/Twin daughters of Tamara and Sean.

*   *   *   *   *

Trina…A Super Child and Sister/Twin to Tamara. Married to Jon.

Jon…A Super Child/Twin to Sean and member of the Security Force. President of the Academy of Magic.

Tristan and **Brendan**…The Second Generation twin sons of Trina and Jon.

*   *   *   *   *

Marigold and **Steele**…Watchers/Nannies to the infant children of Tamara and Sean. New Nannies for Joy.

Pansy and **Cooper**…Watchers/Nannies to the royal children of Trina and Jon.

*   *   *   *   *

Constantine…Tutor to the first-born children of Tamara and Sean and newly appointed Marinean Historian. Taken into custody by the Marinean Security Force for illegal actions at the Academy of Magic.

Crystos…Tutor to the twin girls/Super Sisters born to Tamara and Sean. Super Child and twin to Georgio.

*   *   *   *   *

Terra…Mother of Tamara and Trina, married to Trident; also Head Watcher.

Trident…Father of Tamara and Trina; married to Terra; formerly a Prince and King of Marinea; Ambassador to Alteria. Twin to Trillium.

Trillium…Trident's twin, and Ambassador to Mesarra.

*   *   *   *   *

Savea…A Super Child Sister/Twin to Solange. Married to Verd, son of Tamara and Sean and a Second Generation Super Child. Mother of Lavan and Wavan.

Verd…A first-born child of Tamara and Sean, married to Savea; father of Lavan and Wavan.

Lavan and **Wavan**…Third Generation Super Twins/Brothers; children of Savea and Verd.

Daffi and **Bronze**…Watcher/Nannies to the twin sons of Savea and Verd.

*   *   *   *   *

Mia…Tamara's personal attendant.

Dr. Astarte…Royal Physician to the royal court.

Amanda…Tamara's Social Secretary.

*   *   *   *   *

Dana…Newly-appointed Second in Command and Leader of the Security Force.

Jon and **Borel**…Members of the Marinean Security Force's Special Task Force.

Mimi and **Clark**…New members of the Security Task Force.

Franc and **Kari**…Members of the Force selected to work with the twins to redesign the Practice Sessions.

Georgio…Experienced member of the Security Force and newly appointed tutoring assistant to Constantine in service to the royal children in the Crystal Castle. Once the children became adults, he was appointed as interim Ambassador to Mosshire and interim manager of the Academy President's office. He is now a graduate student at the Academy, working on doctoral research. Super Child and twin to Crystos. Wed to Rose.

*   *   *   *   *

Merlynn…Faux Admissions Officer avatar from the Academy of Magic on Marinea (and former Queen Consort to King Scimitar).

Shamous…Owner of **Your Every Wish**, a magical shop on Marinea. New Crown Prince of Kronos, a Super Child/Twin of Rupert II.

Greta…Proprietor of Pro Bono shop, and a Super Child/Twin to Moonstone.

Professor Yexer…Dissident at the Academy of Magic.

Trixie…Ringleader of older female magic students who 'acted out' at the Palace. Newly-discovered Queen-Designate of the kingdom of Starlight and Super Child. Super twin to Arkin.

Arkin…Newly-identified Super Child and Marinean Ambassador Designate to Starlight. Super twin to Trixie.

Moonstone…Newly-identified Super Child and Twin to Greta. New Marinean Ambassador to Starlight.

Stefan…Fellow Graduate student and love interest of Andrea. Ambassador to Marinea from Planet X.

Dr. Hanover…Special Scientific Consultant to the Crown.

Alteria

Trident...Father of Tamara and Trina; married to Terra; formerly a prince and King of Marinea; Marinean Ambassador to Alteria.

Terra...Mother of Tamara and Trina; wife of Trident; also a Head Watcher.

Tomas...Executive Assistant to Trident. Non-Magical Co-Leader of 'New Friends.'

Mimi...Magical co-leader of 'New Friends.'

Fern...A realtor from Alteria and friend of Terra.

Rose...Daughter of Queen Flora III and Ambassador from Timbere to Alteria. Super Child/Twin to Merlynn. Wed to Georgio.

Violet...Executive Assistant to Rose.

Mosshire

Sostor...An ice magic sorcerer on Mosshire; Ruler of the kingdom; a Super Child/Twin to Sunan of Mesarra; has fair skin, blonde hair and very blue eyes like residents of Mosshire. Married to Solange, a Super Child/Sister to Savea.

Solange...Mother of Trident; Grandmother of Tamara and Trina; a Super Child/Twin to Savea. Married to Sostor.

Coral and **Frosti**...Second Generation Super Sister/Twins/Children of Solange and Sostor.

Pansy and Chrome...Watcher/Nannies to the twin girls of Solange and Sostor.

*   *   *   *   *

Rolf...Watcher and temporary ruler of Mosshire; and leader of an insurrection.

Trina...A Super Child and Sister/Twin to Tamara. Married to Jon. Marinean Ambassador to Mosshire.

Georgio...Interim Marinean Ambassador to Mosshire.

Mesarra

Sunan…A solar magic mage on Mesarra; Ruler of the kingdom; a Super Child/Twin to Sostor of Mosshire; has dark hair and eyes like residents of Mesarra.

Merlynn…Sunan's Assistant in establishing an Academy of Magic in Mesarra. Super Child and Sister/Twin to Rose.

Trillium… A Super Child/Twin to Trident and Trident's identical twin; Marinean Ambassador to Mesarra. Married to Delia.

Delia…Trillium's first hire, the Embassy Manager on Mesarra. Married to Trillium.

Carter…Delia's new Assistant.

Claud…Brief Prime Minister of Mesarra.

(On the dark side of Akura)

Primus

Forty…King of the kingdom of Primus (Personal name: **Linc**).

Martine…Member of Marinean Security Force; Marinean Ambassador to Primus.

Viktor…Commander-Designate of the new Seismic Alert Guard.

Aquelle

Scimitar…Former King of the kingdom of Aquelle; masqueraded as a rogue Watcher; sidekick of King Lucas of Brimstone. Now deceased.

Regis…Ruler and former Prime Minister of Aquelle.

Borel…Member of the Marinean Security Force; Marinean Ambassador to Aquelle.

Anna…Tour guide on Aquelle and first Executive Assistant to Borel.

Pieter…Second Executive Assistant to Borel.

Timbere

Flora III...Queen of the kingdom of Timbere; a Super Child and Sister/Twin to Queen Astrid of Seaside.

Rose...Daughter of Queen Flora III; Super Child/Twin to Merlynn. Timberean Ambassador to Alteria. Wed to Georgio.

Brooke...Secretary to Queen Flora.

Talia...Member of Marinean Security Force; Marinean Ambassador to Timbere.

Hazel...Executive Assistant to Talia.

Clark...Magical Co-Leader of the new experimental project in Timbere. Also a member of the Marinean Security Force. Temporary Ambassador to Alteria.

Borys...Non-magical Co-Leader of the new experimental project in Timbere.

Acorn... Owner of the tree-top restaurant.

Brimstone

Lucas...Former King of the kingdom of Brimstone. Wielder of shadow magic. Now deceased.

Lucian...Former government official and elected ruler.

Scimitar...Former King of the kingdom of Aquelle; masqueraded as a rogue Watcher; sidekick of King Lucas. Now deceased.

Merlynn...Admissions Officer of the Academy of Magic on Marinea; Super Child and Sister/Twin to Rose. Declared Queen Consort to King Scimitar at one point. The majority of her life was spent in captivity in Brimstone. Now helping Sunan establish an Academy of Magic in Mesarra.

Exeter...Marinean Ambassador to Brimstone.

Angus...Once Ambassador-Designate to Farmview. Now Deputy Ambassador to Brimstone.

Freedom

(Name of the new undersea kingdom east of Brimstone, populated by refugees from Brimstone)

Cyril…Leader of the kingdom and Super Child/Twin brother of Cyrus. Wed to Candace of Marinea.

Cyrus…A Super Child/Twin brother of Cyril and second-in-command. Wed to Sunny of Marinea.

Seaside

Astrid…Queen of the kingdom of Seaside; a Super Child and Sister/Twin of Queen Flora III of Timbere.

Kalia…Member of Marinean Security Force; Marinean Ambassador to Seaside.

Margo…Kalia's guide in Seaside.

Kronos

Rupert I…King of the Elven kingdom of Kronos, now deceased.

Rupert II…King of the Elven kingdom of Kronos, a Super Child/Twin of Shamous from Marinea.

Shamous…New Crown Prince of Kronos, a Super Child/Twin of Rupert II. Owner of **Your Every Wish**, a magical shop on Marinea.

Damon…Soldier and Tour Guide.

'Bu..bb..les'

Posidon…King of the undersea kingdom of 'Bu..bb..les.'

Shelley One…Daughter of King Posidon, a Super Child and Sister/Twin of Shelley Two.

Shelley Two…Daughter of King Posidon, a Super Child and Sister/Twin of Shelley One.

Dani…Marinean Ambassador to Bu..bb..les.

On another astral plane...

The Crystal Castle

Adele and **Jeremy**...The current Super Beings.

Elsa...Watcher/Guardian at the Crystal Castle.

Rogere...Watcher/Guardian at the Crystal Castle; Trident's biological father.

Elsewhere in the Universe...

Starlight

An alien kingdom on the planet Starbright (once originally known as Starlight). Recently ruled by a King and Queen who were killed in a crash of their airship on Akura. Now succeeded by their daughter, **Trixie,** a Super Child living on the planet Akura. If officially crowned Queen, she will be known as **Queen Moonbeam,** after her mother.

Skort...Prime Minister of Starlight.

Arkin...Original Marinean Ambassador-Designate to Starlight; Super Twin to Trixie.

Beamie...Guide on Starlight who helped Arkin establish his Embassy.

Moonstone...New Marinean Ambassador to Starlight; Super Twin to Greta.

Neero...Leader of the Insurrectionists.

Shine...Embassy Chief-of-Staff.

Scotti...Manager of the Marinean Embassy Residence.

Trone...Leader of the Starlight Resistance.

Starshine

Another kingdom on the planet Starbright. Originally ruled by Queen Bella, who had been imprisoned by the leaders of a military uprising.

Bella…Queen of Starshine.

Malkum…Consort of the Queen.

Crystos…Marinean Ambassador to Starshine; Super Child and Twin to Georgio. Allowed by the Creator Being to remain a Fourth Generation being.

Planet X

The Ruler…As yet unnamed.

Stefan…Ambassador from Planet X to Marinea.

Jaeda…Ambassador from Marinea to Planet X.

First Generation Super Children
(and their home kingdoms)

Female

Solange (Marinea/Mosshire) and **Savea** (Marinea)

Astrid (Seaside) and **Flora** (Timbere)

Rose (Timbere) and **Merlynn** (Brimstone)

Tamara (Alteria/Marinea) and **Trina** (Alteria/Marinea)

Shelley One and **Shelley Two** (Bu..bb..les)

Trixie (Marinea/Starlight) and **Arkin** (male, Marinea/ Starlight)

Greta (Marinea) and **Moonstone** (Marinea and Starlight)

Male

Sostor (Mosshire) and **Sunan** (Mesarra)

Sean (Marinea) and **Jon** (Marinea)

Trident (Marinea) and **Trillium** (Marinea)

Cyril (Brimstone/Freedom) and **Cyrus** (Brimstone/Freedom)

Rupert II (Kronos) and **Shamous** (Marinea/Kronos)

Arkin (Marinea/Starlight) and **Trixie** (female, Marinea/ Starlight)

Georgio (Marinea) and **Crystos** (Marinea)

Second Generation Super Children
(Marinea)

Candace...Princess and Daughter of Queen Tamara and Commander Lockette. Queen-Designate of Marinea. An original Super Child. Wed to Cyril of Freedom.

Skye...Prince and Son of Queen Tamara and Commander Lockette. An original Super Child.

Sunny...Princess and Daughter of Queen Tamara and Commander Lockette. Second in Line of Succession. An original Super Child. Wed to Cyrus of Freedom.

Verd...Prince and Son of Queen Tamara and Commander Lockette. An original Super Child. Married to Savea; father of Lavan and Wavan.

Tristan and **Brendan**...the Second Generation twin sons of Trina and Jon.

(Mosshire)

Coral and **Frosti**...Second Generation Super Sisters/Twins/ Children of Solange and Sostor.

Third Generation Super Children
(Marinea)

Lavan and **Wavan**...Super Twins/Brothers; children of Savea and Verd.

Fourth Generation Super Children
(Marinea)

Leilani and **Andrea**...the new twin daughters of Tamara and Sean.

Crystal Saga Series 3

7– The Saga of Planet X . . .
and Beyond

D. E. Weingand

Prologue

My name is Sean. I'm the Commander of the Marinean Security Force. I am also wed to Queen Tamara and the proud father of four Second Generation children—two sons and two daughters—and two Fourth Generation twin girls.

Tamara and I have been on many very different adventures, but the one we are beginning now is perhaps the most unusual.

We had fostered a troubled student at the Academy of Magic, who was the sole survivor of a crashed airship from the previously unknown planet of Starlight. When a search-and-rescue ship from that planet arrived, she found out that her parents had protected her in an escape ball—and that they were the King and Queen of that planet.

Thus began a series of adventures which introduced us to the universe and a cosmology that differed vastly from the one we had been accepting for all our lives. We have taken many astral journeys investigating her planet—which is now named Starbright because of the second kingdom we discovered upon it. The term Starlight is now limited to her kingdom—and the second kingdom is Starshine.

But our impending adventure is prompted by the explosion which leveled the intended apartment of our oldest daughter, Candace, who had just returned from her honeymoon with her spouse, Cyril, the Ruler of the kingdom of Freedom on the other side of our planet.

As we tried to ascertain who might have been behind that attack, our investigation focused on who had initiated a previous shapeshifter attack on Tamara and Candace—which now was a very cold case.

With the help of the amazing abilities of our Fourth Generation daughters, we located another previously unknown planet light years away from us and initiated an astral journey to find it. On that journey, besides ourselves, were our daughters, Leilani and Andrea, plus Georgio.

We learned that the star orbited by that planet (which we now call Planet X) is almost at Super Nova stage. The government is trying desperately to find an unoccupied planet to which it can move as much of the population as possible. That is the challenge before us.

When our astral journey to Planet X arrived, we confronted the Ruler—who admitted the previous attack and apologized for it. Given the circumstances that prompted that attack, Tamara was able to forgive their unsuccessful attempt. She also willingly offered our help. We would continue our astral journey to the four planets that had been identified by Planet X's Ruler as possible hosts and assess their suitability.

An interesting aspect of this search is the number of planets: FOUR. Tamara is firmly of the belief that Four has special significance for us; that number has influenced our lives many times.

So now, as we extend our astral journey into this new quest, we are confident—but cautious—that we can be of assistance in this dangerous situation.

Chapter 1
Planet #1

Sean decided to give temporary names to these planets, based on their physical appearances. Planet #1 was very green, with many forests and multiple lakes. He suggested that Bluegreen might be an appropriate name. As they flew around it, they detected no signs of civilization.

Tamara asked our twin daughters to extend their Fourth Generation senses outward. There needed to be certainty that the planet was not home to anyone—and that the air and water were pure.

Tamara also suggested looking for intel concerning the flora and fauna. Were there any hostile elements that might prove dangerous to the Planet X pioneers?

As the girls scanned the surface, they decided to fly lower so their senses could function at maximum reliability. Skimming the treetops, an unexpected danger occurred. Even though their astral bodies were invisible, the vegetation was somehow aware of their presence.

Sean reminded the girls that they were safe. Nothing could harm their astral bodies. But it was very unsettling to observe the various forms of vegetation trying to grab the twins—no matter how unsuccessful that effort might prove to be.

His attention then turned to the bodies of water that had been seen upon approach. As the twins flew over the lakes and streams, what appeared to be some sort of fish with teeth began to leap into the air—trying, like the vegetation, to attack them.

Clearly, this planet would be a hostile environment facing innocent groups of Planet X pioneers. Tamara began to understand why the planet was apparently uninhabited—or, at least, occupied by sentient elements that were not humanoid.

However, the twins were not satisfied. They indicated that we should be more thorough in our examination of the planet before passing judgment. They decided to change the flight pattern to one of a grid, so that no area of the planet would be overlooked.

As our search proceeded, the behavior of the vegetation continued to be hostile. Moving cautiously within the grid pattern, recording what they saw—the explorers found no indication that this planet would welcome any newcomers.

After a long time proceeding in this manner, the group reached the other side of the planet. The star which had given light to the search was about to slip behind the planet. They were entering the night.

Now the planet seemed to really come alive. There were lights below, but the explorers were unable to determine their source. Dipping lower in their flight, the journeyers tried to figure out what they were seeing.

Andrea suggested that, since the lights appeared to be underneath the water, they should enter the water and investigate what might be below. Since their astral bodies were not at risk, everyone nodded and sank beneath the surface.

What they saw was remarkable. This planet was not uninhabited! There was a city appearing before them—and the lights were from inside the multitude of buildings. One building was larger than the others, so they swam over to it.

Entering the building, they observed humanoid figures with gills, going about their routine lives. Unlike Marinea, where a dome had been constructed over the kingdom—and gills were only evident when the residents swam into the open ocean—this city's dwellers had apparently decided to co-exist with their natural environment.

Wondering how they communicated with each other, Leilani and Andrea held hands and tried to access their thoughts. Gesturing 'thumbs up', they shared their findings with the others.

They had learned that no one felt any danger from those hostile fish that had tried to attack the girls. Although no one in the group had noticed, there was a magical protective shield around the city that kept the residents safe.

Listening to the city dwellers' communications, the twins reported that there were many undersea cities like this one. Long ago, a decision had been made to forsake the surface of the planet and its hostile flora.

Apparently, life under the sea had flourished and the residents were very satisfied with their lives. Leilani told her parents that she and Andrea believed no one from Planet X should disturb the balance between the life forms and the environment that had been successfully established on this planet.

Tamara, Sean and Georgio nodded in agreement with the twins' recommendation. They would dismiss this planet as a possible solution for Planet X and continue their exploration of the three other alternatives.

Soaring to the surface and into the air, they moved away from Bluegreen and began their journey onward to the second closest planet on their list, wondering what they would find.

Chapter 2
Planets #2 and #3

The next closest planet candidate was not far, in terms of light years. With the Fourth Generation abilities of the twin girls, the speed of the explorers increased dramatically. Soon, the planet came into view.

This planet presented a completely different appearance. It was completely covered in clouds, so nothing at ground level could be observed. Leilani chuckled and advised that the only possible name for it would be 'Cloudy'!

Andrea agreed and suggested that sinking beneath the clouds was the obvious approach. Hearing no objection, she began to dive toward the clouds, the rest of the group following close behind.

Since the dense cloud cover filtered out much of the light produced by the star the planet orbited, what could be seen of the surface was definitely diminished. Georgio asked the girls to combine their senses and report what they could detect.

Hovering in place, close to the ground, the girls joined hands and concentrated. A short time later, they confirmed that, directly below, there were lakes and forests—but no sign of any inhabitants. However, they proposed that a grid search pattern be utilized on this planet as well. It was the only sure way to accurately evaluate its prospects.

Nodding, the explorers proceeded to implement the twins' recommendation. After examining the entire globe and discovering no signs of civilization, the girls offered another proposal.

"On Bluegreen, we found that sentient life lived both on the surface and below the waters. That may also be true here. So, let's drop into the various lakes and look there as well."

That proved to be a popular decision. The girls dropped down into the nearest lake, followed by the others. Finding nothing of interest, they moved on to a second lake, and then a third and a fourth. Determined to checkout every body of water on the planet, the girls gradually picked up speed.

At the end of the search, there had been no sign of any inhabitants. But Georgio was not ready to label Cloudy a possibility. There were some scientific tests that needed to be conducted, analyzing the purity of the air and water.

Asking Andrea to assist him, the two scientists proceeded to conduct basic procedures. After doing so, they had come to the regrettable conclusion that neither air nor water would be able to support the lives and dreams of the Planet X pioneers. They must keep looking.

*   *   *   *   *

Two planets inspected and two more to find, the five explorers moved on to locate Planet #3. As they approached it, they were startled to see several active volcanoes. Why would this planet have been on the list? At first glance, it certainly did not look welcoming.

Perhaps it was only this view that seemed problematic; other areas of the planet might be more favorable. Since it was on the list, they would definitely have to check it out. As they had done with the first two planets, the twins joined hands and extended their senses. After all, their home planet of Akura had volcanoes, too.

This planet had extensive mountain ranges, containing numerous volcanoes. The twins also observed several large oceans, vast areas of desert and ice sheets at the poles. The climate seemed quite variable.

However, their powerful senses were picking up sounds—sounds that reminded them of machinery. Could this planet have inhabitants after all?

The sounds led the girls to move closer to one of the mountain ranges. This one did not have volcanoes, but the sounds seemed to be located within the mountains. Allowing their astral bodies to penetrate the closest mountain, Leilani and Andrea found themselves in a large cavern. As the other explorers joined them, they were all surprised to find a subterranean city. Apparently, the Planet X scientists had been totally unaware of it.

As they looked around the city, they were unable to locate any humanoid inhabitants. There were many robots tending to the machines, but no flesh-and-blood beings could be found anywhere.

"Do you think that artificial beings have taken over this world?" asked Tamara.

"It's certainly one possibility," replied Georgio, *"but we need to do a thorough search before accepting that conclusion."*

Once again adopting the grid pattern of searching, the explorers examined the planet at both the surface and underground levels. Finding no living inhabitants, the theory of a planet run by robots began to gain strength.

"So, shall we name this planet 'Robotic'?" asked Leilani, as they stood in the original cavern where the sounds had drawn them.

She suddenly ducked, as a robot began to approach her with what looked like a weapon.

"Sis," laughed Andrea, *"It can't hurt you."*

"But how does it know I'm here?" queried Leilani.

"*It may have capabilities that we are unfamiliar with,*" Andrea suggested. "*At any rate…*" and her words were cut off as the robot turned toward her.

Georgio yelled, "*Abort, abort. Let's get out of here!*" They flew toward the cavern's ceiling and out into the open air. Leaving the planet far behind, they headed for the final planetary option.

Chapter 3
Planet #4

As they hovered over the planet now named Robotic, Tamara asked Georgio once more, *"Do you now believe that the planet we observed as controlled by robots was originally inhabited by non-mechanical beings? If so, what do you think happened to those beings?"*

Georgio pondered the question for some time before responding. *"I can't say for sure,"* he said. *"There no longer appears to be any physical evidence supporting that conclusion—but no evidence exists to suggest another explanation, either. Perhaps the twins could manipulate time to reverse engineer what we know and don't know?"*

"Already done," smirked Leilani. *"We were curious, so we did just that—which may be why the robot started moving toward us."*

"So what did you learn?" asked Tamara.

"We recorded what we saw, Mama," Andrea. *"Some time ago, there were sentient life forms on Robotic; they created both robots and other artificial beings to assist them. However, at one point, those artificial entities became*

sufficiently self-aware, enabling them to overcome their makers and take over control of the planet."

"Could you tell what happened to the original inhabitants?" inquired Sean.

"We were able to record brief segments showing robots leading humanoid beings away—but we could only guess at their fate," replied Leilani.

Tamara felt a chill, hearing this reporting. "I will be compelled to tell Planet X officials that they should give this planet a wide berth. Let's move on to our final planet. I have a good feeling about it, since it is number four!"

*   *   *   *   *

As they approached Planet #4, the star around which it orbited was discharging solar storms. By the time they had reached the surface of the planet, the increasing darkness was turning those storms into beautiful auroras.

"What lovely colors!" exclaimed Tamara. "I want to think of that display as a good omen."

"Let's start our grid pattern search here on the dark side. If there are any inhabitants, we should be able to see some lights," suggested Georgio. Nodding approval, the explorers began to follow their well-practiced routine.

By the time they completed their hunt, with no lights being observed, they were quite comfortable with moving on to the light side of the planet. They descended to an altitude just above the surface and reestablished the grid pattern.

Now that it was daylight, they could easily identify the flora and fauna of this planet. Nothing appeared hostile and, while the others continued to search, Georgio and Andrea repeated their strategy of testing the air and water for purity. All results seemed to be acceptable.

When the entire surface had passed their inspection, they sank beneath the exterior to check out if any underground habitations could be detected. Finding none, they once again rose above the planet, deciding to name it "Winner!"

"*My instincts were correct!*" crowed Tamara. "*The number four really does have special meaning.!*"

"*Then why didn't we start with this planet, Mama?*" asked Leilani.

"*We began with the closest one,*" reminded Sean. "*Even if that planet had been acceptable, we would still have examined all four.*"

"*Now it's time to return to Planet X and give them our findings,*" Georgio stressed. "*They need as much time as possible to relocate their population.*"

*　　*　　*　　*　　*

When they reached Planet X, they found the Ruler supervising the lottery that would decide which residents would relocate to the new planet. Allowing themselves to be seen, Tamara and Sean approached the Ruler. After Tamara summarized what they had learned about the four planets, Sean offered a suggestion.

"Is the Ark capable of making more than one flight?" he asked. "If so, you might be able to transport your entire population."

"Now that you have provided concrete intel," replied the ruler, "that will be a real possibility. There will be no need for us to spend time and resources checking out all four planets. You have done us a great service—and I am profoundly embarrassed to share some intel of my own."

Sean frowned and pressed, "What intel do you have that causes you this profound embarrassment?"

"It has come to my attention that some of the crew who had invaded your planet and kidnapped your Queen and daughter have—without authorization—returned to your planet and committed a hostile act."

Sean placed his arm around Tamara and skewered the ruler with his eyes, "And just what act are you referring to?"

Flushing, the Ruler stammered a reply, "I assure you that my government was not involved in any way. In fact, the perpetrators have been arrested."

In a shaky voice, Tamara asked, "For what, exactly?"

Looking down, the Ruler admitted, "For the explosion that was intended to harm your family. They had hoped to distract you so that another invasion could be mounted—they liked your planet and wanted to occupy it."

Georgio and the twins gasped and became visible. Leilani raged, "And we just put ourselves at risk to help you!" Andrea added, "You are not worth helping, after all!"

Tamara straightened and demanded, in a cold voice, "If you are sincere in your assertion of ignorance about their actions, I demand that you turn them over to us for trial and sentencing."

At that moment, there was a flash of light and Cyril, accompanied by the Security Force members who had been investigating the explosion, appeared. "Your decision, please," she pressed.

The Ruler visibly slumped and ordered that the prisoners be brought to him immediately. They would be taken into custody by this military contingent and arrested for their crime.

Once that occurred, Cyril and the Force placed the prisoners in restraints and vanished.

The Ruler wiped his brow and again apologized profusely.

Tamara, Sean, Georgio and the twins held hands, preparing to end the astral journey. Before leaving, Tamara said in a firm voice, "I accept your apology. We wish you a rapid and successful relocation to your new home. However, if you or anyone from your planet should design any hostile act toward our planet in the future, I assure you that the resulting consequences will be severe."

And they disappeared.

Chapter 4
Mission Completed

Back home, Tamara felt the need to call a meeting of SC/United so that she could bring everyone up-to-date on their astral mission. When all the Super Children had gathered, she and Sean described their mission in detail.

Afterward, Cyril gave a complete report on the official proceedings facing the criminals who caused the explosion on Freedom. The rule of law would be followed precisely, but he expected that the perpetrators would never see any personal freedom again.

Tamara added that she had been contacted by the Ruler of Planet X offering to pay for all damages caused by the explosion. As part of his message, he mentioned that the move to the new planet had been carried out very successfully and he thanked us again for making it possible. Part of his message responded to our curiosity about the habitats that we had noticed beneath the water. He assured me that their occupants had also been moved to the new planet—they were nurseries for newborn residents.

Acknowledging the standing ovation that had followed her words, Tamara hugged Sean and her children. She had special hugs for Cecil and Candace, asking how the progress of rebuilding the destroyed apartment was coming along. They assured her that every effort was being taken to have a new building ready very soon.

Thanking her for her support, they let her know that they would also be looking for a residence in Marinea, since they intended to split their time between the two kingdoms.

Tears in her eyes, Tamara expressed her pleasure at hearing that news. Not to be excluded, the twins jumped up and down with excitement. Having Candace in Marinea part-time would make completing the writing of the second play that much easier!

*   *   *   *   *

Candace met with the twins the next day. She wanted to establish a timeline for the new play that they were writing. The overall theme would be a celebration of individual differences and the benefits that accrued to any culture that welcomed them.

Many pages had already been produced. Candace had prepared a draft timeline that would enable opening night to closely follow the ending of the first play. If that were to be possible, auditions would need to begin very soon.

Not surprisingly, the cast of the first play wanted to be considered for the second. As far as Candace and Sunny were concerned, that was to be automatic. Skye was willing to be the producer again, eagerly awaiting a definite date for the beginning of auditions.

However, the location of those auditions had not been decided. The first play had premiered in Freedom because it was that kingdom's story that would be told. Diversity—a major theme of the second play— was a different matter: That play had been inspired by the 'New Friends' project operating in Marinea and Alteria.

Since Rose was deeply involved with that project, both in Alteria and in her home kingdom of Timbere, where it was being replicated, she wanted to be included in the production of this second play.

Candace and the twins welcomed her involvement and asked her opinion about where to hold the auditions. Rose consulted the Elders of Alteria and they unanimously agreed to host both the auditions and the initial run of the play.

As one of the oldest kingdoms on Akura, Alteria had a lovely Playhouse—one that had offered many plays and performances in its illustrious history. The existence of the Bubble Train enabled Marinean citizens to easily attend performances as well.

Sunny had directed the first play. Now, however, she was very busy with the final offerings of that play in Freedom. In addition, although she and Cyrus had given Shamous free rein on planning their wedding, they couldn't help giving him occasional suggestions.

Consequently, her time was limited, and she was reluctant to embark so soon on another project. After meeting with Candace and the twins, she officially removed herself from consideration as Director of the new play.

Skye couldn't do it. He had already agreed to produce the new play—and, with Greta off-planet, he had total responsibility for the Pro Bono shop.

Rose had an idea. She was deeply involved with 'New Friends' in two kingdoms, so her knowledge of that project was extensive. Her Super Twin, Merlynn, would have access to all that knowledge and experience. Even better, Merlynn's assistance to Sunan in establishing an Academy of Magic in Mesarra was winding down. Rose thought Merlynn would be perfect—and said so.

Candace asked if Merlynn had any training in the theater and Rose laughed. She related examples of Merlynn's life experience as proof of her theatrical abilities—which were innate, not learned in school. The twins agreed, also proposing that they sign on as her interns. Bringing Fourth Generation abilities couldn't hurt!

And so it was decided. All that was needed involved talking to Merlynn and getting her to accept. Candace suggested inviting her to lunch tomorrow. They would ask her to teleport to Alteria and meet them at their favorite cafe.

What could go wrong?

Chapter 5
Meeting for Lunch

Although a table outside was always preferred by Rose, this time she felt that privacy would be an important factor. She selected a lovely large booth in a secluded corner of the cafe. Since Super Twins were always aware of the location of the other, Rose didn't even bother to send Merlynn directions.

Candace, Sunny and the twins arrived soon after Rose, with Merlynn close behind. Once they were all seated and their orders taken, Rose asked Candace and Sunny to briefly summarize their experience with the first play.

They looked at each other and Sunny asked, "How can I BRIEFLY put into words all the joy and enthusiasm we experienced by putting on that play? I've had a lot of great times as an actor, but directing our play has been the highlight of my career!"

"As for me," added Candace, "writing the play was my initial contribution, but what Sunny is describing woke up an acting bug in me and I practically begged to have a role on the stage—which she generously designed just for me! I LOVED being the Narrator!"

Merlynn sighed and wondered, "If you had so much fun, why aren't you doing the second play yourselves? As Rose's Super Twin, I'm aware that you invited me to lunch to see if I could be convinced to pick up the Director's position in this new play."

Flushing, Sunny had to admit the truth of what Merlynn was asking. "It's not because of lack of interest—it's lack of time and a sudden onslaught of new responsibilities in my life. You may not know it, but Cyrus and I are joining our life paths as soon as our first play closes!"

"Ah, then let's make this luncheon a party," proposed Merlynn, "a celebration of your new life direction!"

Rose added, "There's a very important reason why they are asking you and me to join in the planning and presenting of this second play. It is inspired by my 'New Friends' project."

"And as your Twin," Merlynn continued, "I have automatic access to all your knowledge of that program. Makes sense—especially since my project in Mesarra is coming to a close. But, Rose, you must be distracted because you are obviously not aware of what happened last night."

Rose looked confused...and then a bit guilty! "Sis," she gushed, "How wonderful!" She hugged her Super Twin as the others at the table looked perplexed.

"What is happening?" inquired Leilani.

"I don't know," answered Andrea. "Obviously, Rose just tuned into whatever occurred in Merlynn's life last night!"

Holding hands, the twins closed their eyes and grew silent—then they laughed and yelled, "Congratulations!"

Now Candace was puzzled. "Am I the only one who has no idea what is going on?"

"Sorry," apologized Leilani. "We just had to read their minds! Merlynn is engaged!"

"What?" exclaimed Candace. "Who is the lucky man?"

"Sunan, of course," admitted Merlynn. "We've worked closely together on this Academy project and our professional life paths became personal as well."

"Does that mean that you are not interested in becoming Director of the new play?" asked Sunny with a worried look on her face. "I would certainly understand, especially since I used that reasoning myself—but I hope we can still persuade you."

"Since I was aware of your intention," replied Merlynn, "I have already talked it over with Sunan. He is totally supportive. Being able to teleport makes multi-tasking so much easier to handle!"

"Then you accept?" pressed Candace.

"I do," admitted Merlynn, "but I warn you that I will need a lot of help."

Everyone started clapping...the second play had just been launched!

*   *   *   *   *

With Merlynn aboard, the planning team could now schedule auditions. They had already decided to hold them in the theater in Alteria where the play would be staged. The only exception would be for the current cast members of the first play. Since that play had not yet closed, the planning team would hold special auditions in Freedom for them.

Auditions would begin in one moon's time, alternating between the two locations. The total number of roles in the second play would be similar to the number in the first play. Further, because of the overwhelming success of the Narrator role, Candace and the twins had included it in the design of the script for the second play.

There was a substantial semester break at the Academy in Marinea coming soon. Auditions in Alteria would be scheduled for that time period. Auditions in Freedom would be held as time allowed, given the necessary tasks associated with ending the run of play #1.

What the planning team did not realize was that negotiations had been ongoing between Jon and Sunan for some time. An official partnership between the two Academies was about to be finalized.

Chapter 6
The Theater Landscape Changes

As planned, in one moon's time, the auditions would commence in both locations. The official closing of the first play was advertised as being in two moon's time—and then Sunny would be free to immerse herself in wedding planning. Privately, she was so grateful that Shamous had accepted the responsibility of overall wedding arrangements.

It seemed that everyone in the cast of the first play intended to audition for the second. That was a good testimony to the effectiveness of Sunny as a Director. She had definite mixed feelings about not participating in the next play, but her wedding had to take priority.

Sunny tried to explain to Merlynn how all-consuming the duties of the Director could become. Merlynn did not seem bothered, however. She had been working with Sunan for some time to establish an Academy of Magic in Mesarra—which had also been very demanding.

However, since Sunny appeared to be unhappy that she had no role in producing the second play, Merlynn took her hand and suggested: "Have you given any thought to taking over the Narrator role? It was very successful in the first play and should be repeated."

Sunny stared at her, "No. I haven't. I just assumed that Candy would want to do it again."

"Don't assume," advised Merlynn. "Ask her."

*　　*　　*　　*　　*

After the next performance of the play, Sunny took Candace's arm and aimed her at their favorite pub. When they had settled at a table and ordered drinks, Sunny began, "Candy, I have an awkward question to ask you."

"Sunny, there has never been any awkwardness between us. Ask away," Candace replied.

Clearing her throat, Sunny said, "Are you going to audition for the Narrator role in the new play?"

"Is that all?" laughed Candace. "Why do you ask? Ah, are you interested?"

Flushing with embarrassment, Sunny had to admit that she was. "I am," she admitted. "I had to turn down the Director position because of its time commitment, but I think I could handle the Narrator role—not that it was an easy one. You did a great job and will be hard to follow!"

Candace smiled and hugged her sister. "You're tying yourself in knots, Sis. Relax. I didn't plan to audition. My focus needs to be elsewhere."

28

"What are you planning?" inquired Sunny. "What don't I know?"

Candace took Sunny's hand and placed it on her abdomen, "As Generation 2, we can't read minds, but we can share feelings. Focus."

"I feel a throbbing—Candy, you're with child!" exclaimed Sunny.

"I thought you might be able to tell," Candace sighed. "Don't tell anyone. I haven't told Cyril yet!"

Sunny hugged her sister and promised to keep her secret. But she whispered, "Candy, you were just wed! Are you sure?"

"I am," Candace answered, "I can already communicate with her. By the way, it was a wonderful honeymoon!"

Laughing, Sunny agreed. "Apparently so! When are you going to tell Mama and Da?"

"I'm planning to let Cyril know tonight—then I'll teleport to Marinea tomorrow," Candace promised.

The sisters hugged once more and proceeded to enjoy the evening.

*   *   *   *   *

Candace did what she had promised. Cyril picked her up and danced across the room; he was so excited! The next day, when Candace shared the news with her parents, they were also pleased—and a little surprised since the wedding had only been a few weeks ago. When Tamara asked if she was sure, she gave the same response that she had given Sunny: "I already communicate with her!" Tamara looked at her daughter and asked, "What did you just say?" Candace repeated herself and Tamara hugged her. "I have never been able to connect with my children before they were born. How amazing!"

"Really, Mama?" inquired Candace. "It feels so normal to me. I wonder if Lavan and Wavan talked to Savea before they were born. Maybe it's a Third Generation gift."

Tamara vowed to visit Savea and find out. She was intrigued.

*   *   *   *   *

The same day, Tamara mentally sent a message to Savea asking when it would be convenient to visit. She received an immediate reply: "Any time. How about now?"

Smiling, Tamara took Savea at her word and teleported into Savea's undersea home. Hugging, the two women settled into very comfortable chairs at a table already set for tea and cookies.

"Is this visit purely personal?" asked Savea, "or can I be of help in some matter?"

"Actually, it is both," admitted Tamara. "I've just found out that Candace is with child—a real surprise since the wedding was so recent. When we were chatting, she confirmed her condition by telling me that she and the babe had been communicating! I had never had that experience while carrying any of my children. Have you?"

Chapter 7
Savea's Reply

Laughing, Savea answered, "Sometimes I kind of wondered. While I was carrying the boys, I tended to talk to myself. If they kicked or wiggled, I took that as a response. But I wouldn't call it communication—which does assume meaning."

"Candace intends to talk to the boys herself," Tamara added. "She is wondering if that ability is tied to the babe being Third Generation—which the boys definitely are."

"I'll be interested in what my sons have to say," continued Savea. "If they could understand what I was saying, perhaps we need to explore further. I hope I wasn't being inept!"

"There is another aspect that may or may not be relevant," pressed Tamara. "The length of time you carried the boys within you was unusually brief. I remember being shocked when you suddenly delivered them!"

"So was I," agreed Savea. "I expected a much longer period of gestation—and then, suddenly, Dr. Astarte was assisting in the birth!"

As the two women continued to enjoy their tea and cookies, a flash of light announced the arrival of Candace and the boys. *"Oh my,"* Savea privately shared with Tamara, *"This should be interesting!"*

Lavan grabbed the plate of cookies and shared them with Candace and his brother. Wavan produced three additional chairs so that they could also be seated at the table.

"Mama," began Candace, "the boys and I have been talking about the possibility of pre-birth communication. Wait until you hear what they have to say!"

Tamara and Savea exchanged looks. *"I can hardly wait!"* commented Savea privately. The boys each took one of Savea's hands. Wavan spoke first, "Mama," he said, "we could hear your words when you thought you were talking to yourself."

"We tried to answer you," added Lavan, "but you didn't seem to hear us."

"We tried to get your attention by kicking and moving around," continued Wavan.

"But nothing seemed to work," concluded Lavan.

"So we agreed to speed up our pre-birth development," added Wavan. "That is why we were born early."

Savea's jaw dropped; she had never heard of such a

thing. "How could you do that?" she stuttered, "I didn't know that was possible!"

"Haven't you wondered why we were born so early?" inquired Lavan.

"Of course," admitted Savea, "but I'm just astonished that you were able to control the natural birth process."

"Actually," added Candace, "I believe what they did was manipulate Time. It would seem that ability surfaced first with the Third Generation and not the Fourth, as we had assumed."

Tamara put her hands to her temples and sighed, "My head is starting to hurt again!"

"Mine did, too, Mama," said Candace, "when the boys first told me what they had done. I think we're going to have to come to terms with an emerging group of children who will have this capability. I fully expect my babe to be next— although, since we can actually communicate, she may not feel the need to speed up her birth."

"I suggest you alert Crystos to this new development. He has the responsibility of tutoring new Fourth Generation beings, but this ability is so important that he may have to add Third Generation to his to-do list!" advised Tamara.

"Good point, Mama," praised Candace. "I'll be sure to let him know."

Kissing their mothers farewell, Candace and the boys teleported out.

Savea stood and walked to a sideboard which was used to serve drinks. "I think we need something stronger than tea!" she said.

Tamara nodded and sank back in her chair. "Now we have to inform our spouses of this amazing discovery."

"Indeed," agreed Savea, "Over a glass of wine!"

*   *   *   *   *

Crystos had not as yet assumed his post of Ambassador to the kingdom of Starshine. Political 'difficulties' had not as yet been resolved. In the meantime, he was continuing his studies at the Academy of Magic in Marinea.

He was spending a lot of time in the library of the Security Force and consulting with Georgio when their interests intersected. When Candace sought him out, this was where she found him.

Pulling up a chair, she began to relate what she had just learned from Wavan and Lavan. As a newly authorized Fourth Generation being, he found her narrative compelling.

"I certainly agree with Tamara that I should oversee the Third Generation as well," he stated. "If unaware Third Generation children were to just stumble upon this ability, there could be chaos."

"I'm relieved that this all came to light before my babe is born," asserted Candace. "I think we are fortunate that Wavan and Lavan have good hearts and positive ethical compasses."

"I agree," Crystos affirmed. "However, I think I had better have a chat with them sooner, rather than later."

"May I be present?" asked Candace. "I am carrying a Third Generation babe that is quite a communicator."

Smiling, Crystos took her hand and they teleported to join the boys.

Chapter 8
The First Meeting

"How did you know where to find them?" asked Candace.

"I'm constantly discovering new Fourth Generation Abilities," Crystos related. "This is one of the most recent. It comes in very handy."

They were standing at the entrance to a local cafe. Lavan and Wavan were sitting at an outdoor table, enjoying mid-afternoon drinks and refreshments. They were sharing the table with Leilani and Andrea, Candace's Fourth Generation twin sisters—and the first to display Time manipulation abilities.

Walking over to the table, Crystos and Candace pulled over two more chairs and sat down. Crystos immediately took charge. "We need to talk," he said.

The two sets of twins looked confused. Lavan questioned Crystos, "About what? And what are you doing here?"

"My name is Crystos," he began. "I was the tutor to your cousins, Leilani and Andrea. The Creator Being upgraded me to Fourth Generation, originally only for the duration of my tutoring—but then extended it indefinitely. I was given the charge to tutor all Fourth Generation beings as they appeared.

"However," he continued, "I have just learned that you, the Third Generation, have used a power that we thought was originally given only to the Fourth Generation: the ability to manipulate Time."

Leilani and Andrea stared at their cousins, exclaiming, "You can do that, too? We thought we were the only ones— until Crystos found that he could do it as well!"

Lavan and Wavan flushed and admitted that, indeed, they had used that power before being born. "But we haven't used it since," they protested.

"I'm relieved to hear that," continued Crystos. "This power could cause chaos. It will be my duty to tutor all four of you in the responsible usage of the ability."

Crystos then proceeded to negotiate a reasonable schedule for his tutoring. The girls seemed to appreciate this new opportunity; the boys were less amenable. Noticing their reluctance, Crystos assured them that learning how to use the ability appropriately would be beneficial to them in the long run.

The girls offered their support, telling their cousins how much they had enjoyed Crystos' tutoring over the years. Finally, the boys agreed to participate, and the schedule was approved.

"Now let's enjoy some refreshments and you can talk about your experiences with this very significant ability," suggested Crystos.

*   *   *   *   *

After the two sets of twins had shared how they had used Time, they stared at each other in awe. The boys stressed that they had only manipulated Time in order to hasten their birth. The girls, however, had creatively caused Time to provide longer opportunities for writing the second play script. Their productivity at both the Academy and with writing the play had significantly improved.

Crystos summarized the discussion by pointing out that Time periods could be changed for many possible reasons. This was why it could be a beneficial ability—or one with the potential to have dire consequences. Both sets of twins nodded their understanding and promised to take his tutoring very seriously.

*   *   *   *   *

When the refreshment break was over, Crystos and Candace decided to take a walk. "Do you think I convinced them?" asked Crystos.

"I do," replied Candace. "They are very smart and I believe they have a new realization of what could happen if that ability were used without due consideration of potential consequences. I can see why the Creator Being extended your Fourth Generation status."

"Thank you for your support," Crystos added. "I'm actually pleased to be needed as a tutor again; I really enjoyed tutoring the girls."

"And now you have to balance it with your coming duties as an Ambassador," Candace reminded him.

Teasing, he chuckled, "At least I can extend Time if I begin to run out!!!"

Clutching her belly, Candace grimaced, "Your newest student seems to object to your humor!"

"I'll try to be more professional when in her presence," he promised. "Oh my, do you think she has overheard the boys talk about hastening their birth?"

"I'm afraid so," Candace admitted. "She and I will have to discuss this further."

"Can you really do that?" asked Crystos.

"Absolutely," Candace affirmed. "That's why I was so certain that I was with child."

"How amazing," praised Crystos. "I feel like I must caution you: Don't be too sure that your babe will be Third Generation. I'm sensing more advanced abilities."

Chapter 9
The Play Progresses

It was time to hold the auditions for the second play. Deference was given to the cast of the first play; they had much to do as the first play prepared to close. The first week of auditions would take place in Freedom. Then the Evaluators would relocate to Alteria.

Skye, Sunny, Merlynn and Candace comprised the Evaluation Committee. Sunan asked for—and was granted—permission to observe the process.

While the auditions were being scheduled, Merlynn and Sunan took time to sit down with Skye and Sunny to discuss the mechanics of producing a play. Since Merlynn had no prior experience as the Director of a play, she was very grateful for the advice she was hearing. Skye recommended that a Production Manager be hired to oversee the technical aspects of the play, to be supervised by Skye. Everyone agreed.

*   *   *   *   *

The first day of auditions in Freedom had arrived. Since most of the candidates had performed in the first play, the Evaluators looked forward to a very pleasurable time.

The level of talent was extraordinary. It was so good that Merlynn decided to create a chart of the roles to be filled, leaving room for the names of possible actors at one side.

As the hours and days counted down, it soon became evident to Merlynn that this play might turn out to be a repertory theater. All of the actors from the first play that auditioned were somewhere on her chart.

She called a meeting of the Evaluators at the end of the week, sharing her chart and personal conclusions with them. It soon became obvious to everyone that the auditions in Alteria would supplement the data on Merlynn's chart.

As was the situation with the first play, additional Directors for the prospective touring companies were also submitting resumes. However, no name popped up for the position of Production Manager. Merlynn was quite concerned about that.

Skye took her arm and led her into a secluded area of the theater. "You have worked closely with Sunan for a lengthy period of time," he began. As she nodded, he continued, "How well does he manage his kingdom?"

"Extremely well," she replied. "He is a very capable administrator and knows when to delegate a project."

"Would you say he had any free time?" pressed Skye.

"Sometimes," she replied. "Why do you ask?"

"Because I think we should consider him for the Production Manager position if he is willing," explained Skye.

"Of course!" she exclaimed. "Why didn't I think of that? And we work so well together. I hope we can persuade him."

"He is obviously interested in the play," added Skye, "or he wouldn't have asked to observe. Let's talk to him."

*   *   *   *   *

Skye and Merlynn returned to the main theater in search of Sunan. They found him chatting with Sunny. Merlynn asked, "Could we have a moment, Sunan?"

Nodding, he followed them to a more private area. Merlynn summarized the conversation that she and Skye had just finished. She looked at Sunan and tried to understand the emotions on his face.

The mystery was solved when Sunan picked her up and twirled around. "I'd be honored to be involved with this wonderful play!" he exclaimed. "I've been grieving inside that our Academy project was drawing to a close. Now I'll have another opportunity to work with you, Merlynn. I'm so happy!"

Hand in hand, followed by Skye, Sunan and Merlynn rejoined the other Evaluators. Sunny congratulated Sunan on his new position as Production Manager—admitting that Super

Children also had Super Hearing! "You can't keep secrets from us!" she crowed.

* * * * *

Now that the auditions in Freedom had ended, the Evaluators—including Sunan as a new member—relocated to the kingdom of Alteria. They had met for breakfast in order to all be on the 'same page' for the first day of auditions at the Playhouse in Alteria.

As they approached the Playhouse, they were stunned to see a very long line waiting outside. "Oh my," Sunny sighed. "There's so much interest here. How will we accommodate everyone?"

Candace opened the door and ushered the Evaluators inside. "I think we need to rethink our original parameters for this second play.

"Merlynn, you may need to revise your chart to reflect what we decide." Walking down the aisle, Candace led the way to seats near the front of the main floor.

"I have one proposal to consider," Candace began. "We had thought about making this play a repertory offering. That is still certainly possible. But now that there are so many actors showing interest, perhaps we should be transparent about the auditions—announcing that they are for the Alterian Playhouse—AND for a group of touring companies. That would give Merlynn the flexibility to rearrange actors and locations where it would make the most sense."

"I LIKE that idea, Candy!" cried Sunny. "Certainly, there is nothing sacred about the design of the first play. Creativity is always a good move."

The rest of the Evaluators nodded their approval and Merlynn enthusiastically supported the flexibility she had just been granted!

Chapter 10
The Second Play

Excitement was building! The auditions in Alteria resulted in a large number of acceptable actors. Merlynn could already see that a resident company—PLUS a host of touring companies—was possible. Only the logistics needed to be worked out.

One unanticipated benefit particularly drew her attention: the large number of applicants seeking to be Directors of the touring companies. Clearly, this second play would have wide exposure.

She was pleased that Sunan had agreed to come aboard. They had worked so closely together in Mesarra and she had shared his regret about that project coming to an end. Their developing personal relationship had definitely enhanced the professional one.

The negotiations between Sunan and Jon were now completed. The model Academy that she and Sunan had created in Mesarra would be the template for potential Academies developing around the planet. She hoped that Mesarra was only the beginning. Future expansion of the

Academy of Magic and its descendants would rest in the very capable hands of Jon, with Sunan as a consultant.

Now that Mesarra was in the rear-view mirror, Merlynn could focus all her energies on directing the play in Alteria. It had just come to her attention that the script being produced by Candace and her twin sisters was nearly finished. The play was about to shift into high gear!

*   *   *   *   *

Sunny felt like a weight had been lifted from her shoulders. The auditions had now been completed and Merlynn was busy assigning roles to the successful applicants. Sunny's final contribution would be to advise Merlynn in that endeavor.

Roles in both the Resident Playhouse and Touring Companies would need to be filled. The Directors hired for the Touring Companies would participate in the final selection of actors for those roles.

Sunny would have no difficulty working the Narrator role in the second play into her schedule. Her primary responsibility would be two-fold: directing the final performances of the first play in Freedom, including the related festivities; and completing the plans for her wedding to coordinate with the Touring Company play's final performance in Marinea.

Thinking about those responsibilities reminded her to contact Shamous. Even though she and Cyrus had technically delegated the wedding decisions to him, she still felt like she wanted their ideas to be part of the process.

*   *   *   *   *

When Sunny and Cyrus walked into his shop, Shamous was not surprised. He had thoroughly enjoyed creating the design for their wedding, but he had left room for what would inevitably come: the input from the bride and groom!

Shamous effusively welcomed the couple to his shop. He congratulated them once again on their upcoming nuptials. Sunny blushed and stammered, "Shamous, I know we gave you full control over the preparations, but we do have a few ideas."

Laughing, Shamous escorted them over to a nearby couch and admitted, "I knew you would. I have been waiting for you."

Cyrus looked stunned, "You have? You expected us to change our minds?"

"No," began Shamous. "I anticipated that you would want to put your own desires into the process. Let's start with my summary of what has already been put into motion."

He then waved his hand and created a large vid screen. Another wave and an animated succession of colorful images filled the screen. Sunny and Cyrus gaped as they recognized themselves on the screen—getting married!

They viewed themselves taking final bows at the conclusion of the closing performance of the play in Freedom, then raising glasses in a toast at the after-party.

The next images were of Cyril and Candace joining them on the stage, arriving in a hot air balloon. Other balloons suddenly appeared on stage—containing the rest of the bridal party.

As Sunny and Cyrus sat in awe, the balloons faded from view, replaced by empty balloons ready to accept new passengers. Each balloon contained a Super Child pilot, capable of teleporting to the next location: Marinea.

Finally, a lavishly decorated bridal balloon appeared and the images of Sunny and Cyrus—now attired in bridal finery in shades of yellow and orange—entered it. Terra, who would be the celebrant, would teleport this final balloon.

The images dissolved and, when more appeared, the locale had clearly changed to the sky above the outdoor theater in Marinea. It was filled with many balloons: the ones that had just teleported from Freedom.

As the balloons settled on the ground, their occupants exited and walked toward the outdoor stage where the Touring Company had just taken final bows. When they had taken their places on the stage, an orchestra appeared in front of the stage, playing the music from the first play and smoothly shifting to the score of the second play. A trumpet fanfare announced the arrival of the bridal party and additional balloons appeared in the sky.

When the balloon containing Sunny and Cyrus was seen, the wedding guests stood and applauded loudly. After landing, the bridal pair walked together down a path of orange blossoms toward the stage. Terra had teleported directly to the stage and awaited them there.

At the conclusion of the ceremony, several large tents materialized on the surrounding grass. Elves escorted the wedding guests to the tents and other elves roamed around, offering refreshments. Since the cast of the first play had also been hired for the second, the transition between plays was complete.

Chapter 11
Finalizing Plans

Sunny and Cyrus were overwhelmed! They gazed at each other and giggled. "Shamous, you are amazing!" exclaimed Sunny. "We had some suggestions, but you have already incorporated them into your design!

"We had asked you to have the wedding at the conclusion of the first play—and you did!" she added. "But I was yearning to also be wed at home in Marinea—and you managed to do both!"

Cyrus shook Shamous' hand and congratulated him on a brilliant design. "We won't ask you to change a thing!" he vowed. "Everything we just witnessed is perfect!"

Shamous beamed with pleasure. He had hoped that they would like most of his design—but they loved all of it! He smiled and then asked, "Would you like to see your actual wedding garments?"

Nodding happily, Sunny and Cyrus accepted bubbly drinks from an elf who had just entered with a tray full of refreshments.

Shamous added one more comment, "Since you have

approved my little vid show, I will have copies available for all your guests as mementos of your special day."

Sunny put down her drink, stood and gave Shamous a huge hug. "I think you are our Fairy Godfather!" she exclaimed. Shamous flushed and replied, "It was my pleasure!"

*   *   *   *   *

It was the day of the wedding of Sunny and Cyrus. It was also the final performance of the first play, in Freedom and with the Touring Company in Marinea. The bride and groom were nervous about both events, even though the preview produced by Shamous in his shop had given them a complete picture of how the day would proceed.

Candace and Cyril greeted them at the theater in Freedom. No one would change into bridal finery until the intermission of the play. The audience had been advised that the length of the intermission would be extended—and that drinks were on the house! Shamous had hired special entertainment and everyone in the audience was aware of the wedding to come.

When the intermission arrived, the bridal party entered a special area provided by Shamous where they could change into their bridal attire. A private nook was designed for the bride so that her gown would remain unseen until the bridal balloon arrived in Marinea. To allow her to join in the final curtain applause, Shamous had cloaked her in a white cape secured by magical ties. He wanted the surprise to be total after she teleported into Marinea. Not even Cyrus had actually seen her in her dress.

When the play resumed after intermission, there was a heightened level of anticipation in the audience. The final curtain dropped to a roar of thunderous applause and a standing ovation. After all bows were taken, Sunny and Cyrus returned to center stage.

Cyrus presented her with a huge bouquet of flowers and she looked at him lovingly as she thanked the audience for their patronage and urged them to continue their support when the second play opened—which would be soon. Everyone raised their glasses in a toast to the transition between plays—and the wedding that celebrated it!

The bridal hot-air balloon appeared, and they stepped aboard. As other balloons joined them, the bridal balloon lifted into the air and vanished, followed by the others one-by-one. It was a grand finale!

*   *   *   *   *

In Marinea, the wedding guests who were not present at the final play performance in Freedom had begun to gather at the outdoor theater. As trumpets sounded, their eyes looked up to the sky. A parade of hot-air balloons began to appear, depositing guests on the lawn.

Elven ushers started to escort them to seats in the theater. Once everyone was inside, another trumpet fanfare announced the arrival of the bridal party. The first balloon contained the family of the groom; the second, the family of the bride.

The next balloon deposited the witnesses, who walked on a path of orange blossoms into the theater. The final balloon contained the bride and groom, who stepped out of the balloon and followed along the path. As Sunny's feet touched the path, her white cloak disappeared and her glorious yellow and orange bridal gown could be seen. Cyrus gazed at her in awe and, hand-in-hand, they entered the theater, where Terra awaited them on the beautifully adorned stage.

The wedding and the reception to follow were about to begin!

*   *   *   *   *

Shamous' design of the wedding day was so elaborate and innovative that, once the newlyweds had departed, the 'afterward' almost came as a relief! Tamara and Sean had returned to the Palace and were enjoying a beverage in the garden. "Three of our original four children have now shared their life paths," commented Sean. Tamara nodded and said, smiling, "Now I'm waiting for Skye to join them!"

Chapter 12
A Message From Planet X

The second play was about to open in Alteria. The historic Playhouse had welcomed many plays, but this one was unique in many respects. It had never been performed before, and the authors were royalty from a neighboring kingdom. Candace, Leilani and Andrea had worked diligently to complete the script, aided by the magic inherent in the Fourth Generation twins.

Now that their responsibility as playwrights had ended, Leilani and Andrea were free to focus on their Graduate studies. They intended to remain connected to the evolution of the play, but having that phase of their lives no longer driving the content of their lives was a relief.

That welcome feeling was short-lived, however. What was to replace it was totally unexpected.

*   *   *   *   *

Leilani was hurrying across campus; she was running late for her meeting with her twin. They had agreed to share a drink at their favorite cafe. As she neared her destination, she saw that Andrea was not alone.

She frowned because she did not recognize the man sharing Andrea's table. As Super Twins, she expected to share every facet of her sister's life. Who was this guy?

Reaching her sister's table, she pulled out a chair and looked at her twin quizzically. Andrea flushed with embarrassment and sent a silent message of apology; she had been keeping this aspect of her life private.

Andrea opened her mind to Leilani, allowing her to fully share the connection with Stefan, the man sitting next to her. He was a Graduate student, enrolled in advanced science courses with Andrea. They had apparently become close over the semester, and that connection seemed to be strong.

Leilani allowed her senses to subtly explore his mind; she needed to satisfy herself that his intentions and moral core were worthy of her sister. Andrea's eyes widened as she became aware of her sister's action, but she sighed and did not object. Leilani's love was unconditional, and she was entitled to be concerned about Andrea's welfare.

Andrea relaxed as she sensed Leilani's concern subside. However, there was another exploration happening—Stefan was also extending his senses to search Leilani! Andrea immediately inserted a block to protect her sister's privacy.

"What is going on?" demanded Andrea, staring at Stefan. Stefan shrugged and replied, "I figured that if she wanted to scan me, I would return the favor."

"How did you know to do that?" Andrea protested. "That's an advanced ability. We haven't talked about magic and powers; I think it's time."

The two sisters stared at Stefan, mentally probing for a response. He smiled, but stayed silent. His lack of transparency disturbed the twins, who wondered what he was trying to conceal.

At that moment, Candace approached their table. Grabbing a vacant chair, she positioned herself as an observer. A minute later, Skye appeared and produced another chair. Stefan looked around, his smile faltering.

"Have I done something wrong?" he asked.

"I don't know—have you?" inquired Skye.

Andrea was clearly uncomfortable. She had been having an enjoyable break from classes with a friend—and now it felt like an entirely different experience: an inquisition!

Candace had an eerie feeling that she knew this man— but she couldn't recall from where. The babe in her womb turned and kicked—and she suddenly remembered! "Where are you from?" she asked pointedly.

"Who are you and why do you want to know?" Stefan insisted.

"We're family," Skye replied. "Please answer the question."

Stefan began to stand, but some vines appeared and forced him back into his chair. Attempting to free himself, he discovered that the vines became tighter.

"Candy," pressed Skye, "what have you remembered?"

Her face grew pale as she explained, "He was one of the crew who kidnapped Mama and me. I never completely forget faces."

Andrea gasped and grabbed Leilani's hand for support. "Stefan," she cried, "Is she correct? Please tell me!"

Hanging his head, Stefan admitted the truth of the situation. "I was sent here to become a friend to you; I have a message for your mother."

"Why all the subterfuge?" asked Skye. "You could have just made an appointment."

"I was afraid of her reaction," Stefan offered. "It was a frightening experience for both the Queen and her daughter."

Skye seized Stefan's arm and they vanished. Candace remained with her sisters to lend her support. Andrea was trembling and her sisters moved to hold her. Candace chanted softly and the trembling eased.

Chapter 13
Resolution

Meanwhile, Skye and his captive appeared in Sean's office. He sent a mental message to his mother to join him there. She arrived within minutes. "What is happening?" she asked. Skye briefly summarized what had occurred at the cafe and secured Stefan in an available chair.

Sean began his special interrogation, with the vid screen above Stefan's head. Stefan was clearly nervous, but began to verbally state the message he had been sent to transmit. When he was finished, he slumped back in the chair, clearly spent.

Tamara looked at Sean and asked, "So the Ruler wants to establish diplomatic relations with us. What do you think?"

Sean thought a moment and replied, "You and Candace were the victims in that first invasion. I'll support whatever response you are both comfortable with. Can you put that trauma aside and chart a new direction?"

"Candace and I will have to discuss this message," Tamara decided. Turning to Stefan, she said, "Tell the Ruler that I am taking his request under consideration. What are your instructions for replying to him?"

"If your response is favorable," Stefan began, "I will be allowed to continue my studies here at your Academy of Magic and assume the post of Ambassador. If it is not, I must return home."

"I will try to give you my decision promptly," promised Tamara. "In the meantime, you will remain in custody here in the Palace."

Tamara turned and left the office, leaving a confused Stefan in her wake.

*   *   *   *   *

Sending Candace a mental message, Tamara learned that she was still with her sisters at the cafe. Deciding to honor her promise of a prompt decision, she teleported to their location.

She was pleased to note that her daughters did not show any signs of discomfort or unease. However, the three of them stood and moved to hug their mother tightly. As they sat down once again, Tamara reported what had happened in Sean's office. Looking closely at Candace, Tamara asked for her feelings about the request that Stefan had brought.

"As you have been describing it," Candace replied, "I've been mentally regarding it through the lens of my Queen-Designate role. It was definitely an upsetting experience for me, but viewing it as a Queen brings a different interpretation to mind.

"Since we actually helped the Ruler in his search for a new planet home—and he was appropriately grateful, and apologetic for the invasion/kidnapping—I think we can accept his offer on a trial basis. Diplomacy isn't always a win-win situation, but the lack of it is definitely a loss for everyone concerned," concluded Candace.

Tamara smiled at her daughter with pride, thinking once again what a great Queen she will make. Leilani and Andrea were gazing at their big sister in awe, obviously having similar thoughts.

"Thank you, dear, for your candor," Tamara commented, "and for your wisdom. I will let Stefan know our positive response. He will be pleased—and also very happy because he will be Planet X's Ambassador here, as well as a student at the Academy." As she spoke, she couldn't help noticing the look of relief on Andrea's face. She'd have to keep an eye on that.

*   *   *   *   *

That evening, Tamara gathered all her children in the Private Dining Room for dinner. Sean had released Stefan from custody and allowed him to communicate with his Ruler. Now it was her responsibility to name someone as Ambassador from Marinea to Planet X.

As part of the dinner conversation, Tamara brought up the subject and asked for any recommendations.

"Actually, I do have one, Mama," offered Andrea. "In one of the classes that Stefan and I have taken together, there was a girl named Jaeda who is friendly with both of us. She is also a very good swimmer, which might be a useful skill, considering the shape-shifting population of Planet X."

"Are you sure you're not trying to remove competition from the playing field?" teased Leilani.

Blushing, Andrea poked her sister and cried, "NO. I wouldn't do that. I'm being serious."

"In that case," responded Tamara, "See if she might be interested. If she is, have her talk to your father and make a formal application."

Nodding, Andrea poked her sister again and began to eat her dinner.

*   *   *   *   *

The next day, Sean presented an application from Jaeda for the Ambassador position. "I think she's a good candidate," he commented to Tamara. "Let me know your opinion."

After examining the application, Tamara told Sean that

she approved. "Have Jaeda talk to Stefan about the logistics of moving to Planet X. Our Ambassadorial corps is clearly expanding—as is our international and inter-galactic influence. This is an exciting—and challenging time," she exclaimed. I wonder what the future holds for us next?"

Crystal Saga Series 3

8 – What's Next?

D. E. Weingand

Prologue

My name is Candace. I am one of the four first-born children of Queen Tamara and Commander Sean of Marinea. I am also the Queen-Designate and will become Queen when my mother decides to relinquish the throne. My hope is that many, many moons will have come and gone before that day arrives.

I have recently wed my soulmate, Cyril, the Ruler of the kingdom of Freedom on the other side of our planet, Akura. We are both Super Children and Cyril is also a biological twin—and a Super Twin—to Cyrus, who is second-in-command in the government of Freedom. Cyril and Cyrus have agreed to switch roles at the point when I become the actual Queen of Marinea.

My personal interests lie in the areas of literature and poetry. I wrote the script for the first play produced in Freedom, based on that kingdom's history. My sister, Sunny, was Director. I became 'bitten' by the 'acting bug' while doing so—and Sunny created the role of Narrator for me. I thoroughly enjoyed that experience!

Since audiences loved that role, we made sure that it was carried over into the second play—which has been written by me and my twin younger sisters, Leilani and Andrea. I should mention that the twins are also Super Children—but are Fourth Generation, whereas I am Second Generation.

Because of changes in her life—one of which is a wedding to Cyrus!—Sunny has declined the Director position on the second play, which has as its theme the advantages of diversity in the population. It is based on the success of the 'New Friends' project on Alteria and Marinea, and replicated on Timbere.

Since Rose, the Ambassador from Timbere to Alteria, has been central to the success of that project—and is the Super Twin of Merlynn, who would have access to all her knowledge and experience—we decided to ask Merlynn if she would accept the Director position.

Thankfully, she agreed!

One of Merlynn's first directives was to ask me to investigate whether Sunny would consider doing the Narrator role—since I was not intending to audition because of changes in my life path. What changes?

Although Cyril and I were only recently wed, I am already with child. Everyone has been surprised. Cyril and I are thrilled, however, and I have been communicating regularly with my daughter—yes, it's a girl!

Apparently, my mother and Aunt Savea were not able to do so before the birth of their children. Upon checking with the twin boys of Aunt Savea, I found out that THEY could hear their mother, but she never responded—which is why they hastened their birth! So now we're guessing that skill had begun with the Third Generation, which is what the boys are.

At last, I understand why my mother's head began to hurt so often—mine is doing the same thing!

Chapter 1
Starting a 'To-Do List'

Now that Candace and Cyril were about to become parents, they decided to create a 'To-Do List' to help them prioritize necessary tasks. They were still living in the official residence of the Ruler on Freedom. Rebuilding the ruined apartment destroyed by the explosion caused by the insurgents from Planet X was definitely a priority. At one point, it was THE most important priority.

However, now that Candace was with child, locating an apartment in Marinea rose to the top of the list. As their daughter's birth grew closer, they would want to be close to Candace's parents and Dr. Astarte.

Which was why they had decided to teleport into Marinea and start looking for an acceptable residence. Leilani and Andrea had offered to do a preliminary search; their ability to extend Time allowed them to do so without having a negative effect on their Graduate Studies.

Since Watchers Marigold and Steele had been hired to once again serve as Nannies to the new royal babe, they were added to the search team. There was one more volunteer, however, who came aboard as no surprise to anyone: Shamous.

Before Candace and Cyril had even arrived, Shamous had dispatched a cadre of Elves to roam the city seeking vacancies near the Palace. Several possibilities had been identified and shared among the members of the search team.

As soon as Candace and Cyril appeared, a royal vehicle scooped them up and Shamous did a drive-by of the properties on the list. He didn't want to tire Candace, so he had created another vid presentation—this time, of the interiors of the properties—which he displayed inside the vehicle.

The royal couple was very impressed and selected three properties to personally visit. Candace remarked that this was the easiest real estate search she could possibly imagine!

After inspecting the three properties, she and Cyril agreed upon a charming three-bedroom home that— surprise!—Shamous had already outfitted with security devices! *"How did he know what we would select?"* wondered Candace.

"We told him," answered Leilani and Andrea, once everyone had reconvened in Sean's office. "It was easy to go ahead in Time to check on your choice."

Sighing, Candace rubbed her temples and welcomed a hug from her mother. *"Mama,"* she communicated privately,

"*I really empathize with your headaches!*"

Shamous inquired, "Would you like to spend the night in your new home? I have decorated it according to your preferences for your wedding; if you wish any changes, that can be arranged at your convenience."

Candace and Cyril couldn't stop giggling; they rose and hugged Shamous and told him that they would be delighted. Meanwhile, Tamara invited everyone involved in the search to join them for dinner in the Private Dining Room. It was time for a party!"

*   *   *   *   *

At dinner, Cyril managed to sit next to Shamous at the table, with Candace on his other side. "Shamous," he began, "would you consider taking over the restoration of our apartment in Freedom? You seem to be uniquely qualified."

A flush of pleasure reached Shamous' face. "You honor me, Sir," he replied. "Let me know when you will be returning home and I will meet you there."

Cyril winked at Candace, privately commenting, "*I think we can cross that task off our 'To-Do List'*." She clasped his hand and responded, "*I definitely agree!*...OH!"

"What is it, dear?" asked Cyril with a worried look.

"Our little girl just informed me that she is ready to be born," Candace answered, wiping her brow. "She feels left out

3

of all the exciting things that are happening!"

"Can't you convince her to be patient?" whispered Cyril.

"I don't think so," Candace sighed. "She learned that it was possible when I brought Lavan and Wavan to talk to Aunt Savea. Oh my!"

"What is happening, dear?" asked Tamara. "You look so pale."

"Mama," Candace moaned, "Would you please send for Dr. Astarte?" and she fainted.

*   *   *   *   *

Candace had been tucked into bed in the classroom in the Palace. Her hope to spend a romantic evening with Cyril in their new home was no longer an option. Dr. Astarte had commandeered Marigold and Steele to help her with the imminent birth.

Cyril was a wreck! A burst of light announced the arrival of Cyrus, who had come to support his twin. Steele advised the brothers to go down the hall to the Chapel. Producing a bottle of spirits, he handed it to Cyrus. "I'll call you when it's time." Cyrus took Cyril by the arm and walked him to the Chapel.

"A few prayers will make Candace feel better," he promised, "and this bottle will help you to feel better as well."

Opening the Chapel door, they walked inside.

Chapter 2
The Birth of Joy

Candace stirred and smiled at Dr. Astarte. "I'm sorry to bother you, Doctor," she sighed. "My babe seems to be in a hurry to be born. I'm afraid it's my fault; she overheard my conversation with Aunt Savea's twins—when they confessed to speeding up their own births."

"Overheard?" asked Dr. Astarte. "Are you telling me that your babe can hear and understand before being born?"

"Absolutely!" Candace asserted. "We've had lengthy conversations from the very beginning. In our most recent chat, she told me she was going to be born soon; she thinks she's missing out on some fun."

Dr. Astarte shook her head in disbelief. "I'm continually amazed at what you children do and say. What is she telling you now?"

"She's very quiet," admitted Candace. "I think she's saving her energy for the birth process—which I think is about to happen soon!" Arching her back, Candace began to pant. Marigold held her hand and started to coach Candace in breathing. Several deep breaths later, a cry could be heard by anyone near the classroom.

Dr. Astarte lifted the babe and swaddled her in a soft blanket. "You're right, Candace. She was definitely in a hurry. And she's lovely! Look at those white curls! I do believe she's smiling at me!"

Candace reached for her daughter as Cyril and Cyrus burst through the door. Kneeling as Candace's side, Cyril kissed her brow and took the hand of his babe. "She grabbed my finger!" he crowed. "I sense that she's going to be a handful!"

Flashes of light occurred all over the classroom as family members teleported in to see the new arrival. A wave of Dr. Astarte's hand and the babe and classroom were cleaned and ready for visitors.

Sunny hugged her sister and asked, "Have you decided on a name?"

Cyril nodded and said, "She's our Joy."

*   *   *   *   *

Candace and Cyril were finally able to move into their new home in Marinea. Shamous had indeed decorated it according to their taste. But when they first entered the building, they tried to remember how the bedrooms had been arranged during their initial visit. They were surprised that there seemed to be differences.

Candace handed the babe to Marigold and asked Cyril, "Wasn't this building two stories? Now there seem to be three floors."

Cyril frowned and admitted, "I think you're right! The first floor had living and dining rooms, plus a large kitchen and guest bathroom. The second floor contained three bedrooms, plus a bath. Now it only has two."

"That's what I remember, as well," said Candace. They noticed, however, that the two bedrooms had also changed. To their delight, Shamous had outfitted one of the bedrooms as a nursery. Located next to the nursery, the second bedroom was clearly intended for the Nannies—and now had a connecting door so the Nannies could easily tend to the new babe. But where was the third bedroom?

Cyril added, "The staircase now goes up to a third floor. Let's check it out." Climbing the stairs, they arrived at a huge suite of rooms: a large bedroom, including an en suite bath, and two smaller rooms that could be used as offices. Everything was perfect!

Candace laughed, "His shop is named '**Your Every Wish**!' He has redesigned our home to reflect OUR every wish! He's amazing!"

Just then, Shamous appeared and inquired, "I hope I have met your needs. If you wish any changes, please let me know." And he vanished.

*   *   *   *   *

The next day, Shamous popped in once more. He wanted to be sure that everything was in order. He found the new parents in the nursery with the Nannies, seemingly listening to what Joy had to say.

"Shamous, I'm so glad to see you!" cried Candace. "You have made this house a true home for us. How can we ever thank you?"

He bowed, saying, "It was my pleasure, Your Highness. Is there anything else I can do for you?"

A cry from the crib caught his attention. Walking over, he smiled at Joy—who smiled back! Candace took his arm and commented, "She was just telling us that she wanted a party so she could meet everybody!"

"TELLING you?" Shamous exclaimed. "She's a babe!"

"True," replied Cyril, "But a very vocal one with a lot of opinions!"

"You can understand her?" Shamous blurted out. "How is that possible?"

"I've been communicating with her regularly from the very beginning, before she was born," admitted Candace. "She decided to be born early because she felt like she was missing a lot of fun! The party is her idea!"

"Then a party she shall have," agreed Shamous, wiping his brow.

Chapter 3
The Party

Invitations were distributed by Sean's birds. There would be an Open House party at the new home of Candace and Cyril in Marinea in one moon's time. The 'hostess' of this event would be the new babe, Joy, who is eager to meet all the Super Children.

As the date of the party drew closer, Shamous met with Joy's parents and displayed his concept designs. Once again, Candace and Cyril were astonished by Shamous' originality. As Cyril made Joy comfortable on his lap, she suddenly sat up and focused on the designs.

Candace laughed, telling Shamous, "She loves your drawings, but could she also have a special chair to sit on?"

Shamous cleared his throat and asked, "Do you have any idea what kind of chair she has in mind?"

Joy extended her arm and a piece of paper floated toward Shamous. Grabbing it, he was astonished to see an image of a chair that would allow Joy to sit upright. He found that he was having trouble understanding what Joy was capable of. "Your babe is more than just remarkable!" he exclaimed. "I'm overwhelmed!"

Joy reached for Shamous, apparently asking for a hug. He took the hint and cuddled her. A sensation of gratitude and pleasure flowed through him. He stared at her and returned her to Cyril.

"I'll do my best to satisfy her wish," he grumbled and disappeared.

"Poor Shamous!" giggled Candace. "I think he's met his match!"

*   *   *   *   *

It was the day of the party. Candace and Cyril knew that their home could not possibly hold the number of Super Children who would come to the party. But they had total faith that Shamous was up to the challenge.

Shamous had arrived early, bearing the chair that Joy had special ordered. Placing her in it, he smiled when she wiggled into a comfortable position and beamed at him. Her approval washed over him like a gentle breeze. The first Super Children entered the house and were greeted by Candace and Cecil. Joy's smile drew them to her, and they were captivated.

One by one, more guests arrived, and Joy's demeanor welcomed them. Candace noticed that the living room seemed to expand as needed to accommodate the number of Super

Children who had teleported in. Cyril was fascinated by what Shamous had wrought. Joy's party was a rousing success!

When the last guests had left, Candace moved to lift Joy from her new chair. Joy's eyes were drooping with fatigue and a nap seemed to be required. As Candace reached for Joy, the babe disappeared! Crying out for Cecil, Candace raced upstairs to the nursery.

As she had guessed, Joy had teleported into her crib and was sound asleep—with a smile on her face! As her parents watched, Joy grabbed her favorite toy and snuggled into her blanket. Cecil put his arm around Candace and led her from the nursery. Shamous met them in the hall and asked if they required anything.

When they replied that everything was fine; they were heading downstairs to clean up after the party, Shamous informed them that he had seen to that already. Wishing them a good night, he vanished.

*   *   *   *   *

The next day, Tamara and Sean arrived to help with the clean-up—only to find Candace and Cecil enjoying breakfast in the kitchen. Looking around, they could find nothing that required their attention.

Tamara complimented her daughter and son-in-law on a successful party. They laughed and admitted that they didn't deserve any praise. Shamous had taken care of everything!

Cecil waved his hand and two chairs appeared. Once they were comfortably seated, Tamara and Sean found themselves with breakfast fare to enjoy. They remarked about the chair Shamous had provided for Joy at the party; as they did so, the chair suddenly appeared at the table—with a passenger: Joy!

As she smiled at her parents and grandparents, Joy wiggled, and her chair morphed into a chair with a tray. On the tray was a bowl of cereal and Joy was holding a spoon. Digging into the cereal, Joy smacked her lips and nodded in approval.

The adults stared at her in amazement! "She's already eating solid food?" asked Sean.

"Apparently so, Da," replied Candace. "And she definitely wants to be a part of anything that's going on—like breakfast!"

The Nannies rushed into the kitchen, crying that Joy wasn't in her crib. Stopping abruptly when they spied her eating breakfast, they sighed in resignation. "She's really going to be a handful!" Marigold prophesied.

"I'd put a tracking device on her," warned Steele, "but she would probably disable it!"

"We'll have a talk with her," promised Candace, as Cecil covered his mouth to hide his smirk.

Chapter 4
Enter Crystos

Tamara had sent for Crystos. When he arrived in her Palace office, she waved him to a chair. "I came as soon as I could, Your Majesty," he explained. "I was in the middle of a test at the Academy."

"No problem," Tamara smiled. "I know you have a life. I need to talk to you about Joy."

"Ah," said Crystos. "I was wondering if that was your intent. I enjoyed her party—and she certainly did, too! But there's more, isn't there?"

"Yes, indeed," replied Tamara, and she proceeded to share Joy's sudden breakfast appearance, plus the worry she had caused her Nannies.

"I warned Candace that I sensed advanced abilities in Joy," Crystos offered. "I don't think she's a Third Generation."

"Really?" asked Tamara. "I was afraid of that. How can we control her then? She is progressing at a rapid rate, both physically and mentally."

"May I start tutoring her, Your Majesty, even though she's still a babe?" he inquired. "And would you authorize the

15

twins to work with me? I know they are also in Graduate School, but it may take all three of us to handle her."

Tamara thought for a minute and then nodded, "'Yes' to both questions. Because the three of you can control Time, I don't believe your studies will be negatively impacted."

"And my Ambassadorship?" Crystos pressed.

"That hasn't been activated yet," reminded Tamara. "I haven't received any recent updates from Starshine, so we'll deal with that later."

"Have you discussed my appointment with her parents yet?" added Crystos.

"No," admitted Tamara. "I wanted to check with you first. I will do so now." Her eyes glazed over as she sent a summons to Candace and Cyril, who appeared almost immediately.

Creating two more chairs, Tamara invited them to sit down. Crystos watched their facial expressions as Tamara related the substance of her conversation with him.

"But Mama," spoke Candace, "She's only a babe. Tutoring should begin when she is older."

Cecil took her hand and said, "She's not an ordinary babe, my dear. She's provided a lot of evidence of that. We love her so much, but I think the Queen is making an informed decision here."

16

Crystos reminded Candace of his comment when they were with the Third Generation boys at the cafe. "My impression then is being borne out now—she's AT LEAST a Fourth Generation, and perhaps more."

Candace blanched and lay her head on Cyril's shoulder. "My poor little one," she sighed. "I want what's best for her—but why couldn't she be just a babe for a while?"

Tamara chuckled, "That's what your father and I thought about you and your three siblings, so I understand what you're feeling. Our family is certainly not typical."

"Mama," Candace added, "there's something else. When Marigold and I were giving Joy a bath today, I noticed that she had a crystal on her tummy—like you did."

"Oh my," exclaimed Tamara. "Be sure you keep an eye on those white curls and let me know when they begin to change color."

"Crystos," Candace inquired, "Shall I tell the Nannies that you are joining our team? After looking at their faces at breakfast, I think they will be happy to have you aboard—and my sisters, as well."

"I think that would be wise, Your Highness," approved Crystos. "Please tell them that I will meet with them in the Classroom tomorrow morning. I still need to alert the twins to this new responsibility."

After exchanging hugs, Crystos bowed to the Queen and vanished.

*   *   *   *   *

Later that day, Crystos found the twins having drinks at their favorite cafe. Pulling up a chair, he ordered a drink and engaged in some small talk.

"OK, Crystos," giggled Leilani, "We know you're not that good with small talk. What's up?"

Leaning back in his chair, Crystos opened his mind to the twins and they gasped! "Wow!" expressed Andrea. "This is huge!"

Crystos nodded. "I agree...and it's a definite challenge."

"Of course, we'll help," Leilani affirmed. "She's our cousin. What Generation do you think she is?"

"It's too soon to tell," admitted Crystos. "Nor do I have any idea why she jumped at least one Generation."

"Do you want us to join you at the Classroom tomorrow morning? We don't have classes," inquired Andrea.

"I think that would be best," agreed Crystos. "We need to woo the Nannies."

"I don't think they'll be a problem," predicted Andrea.

And then Crystos mentioned the crystal.

Chapter 5
The Classroom Meeting

The next day, Crystos and the twins entered the Classroom together. Marigold and Steele were getting Joy dressed for the day and looked up at their visitors. "Candace told us you were coming," began Marigold. "She anticipated that we would welcome your membership on our team—and we definitely do!"

"Yesterday," contributed Steele, "we were alarmed to find Joy's crib empty. After all, she could still be considered a newborn—and our imaginations ran wild!"

"Your fears were quite reasonable," soothed Crystos. "I was sensing that her abilities were far greater than the expected Third Generation ones—and the evidence is mounting that I am correct.

"We must continually remind ourselves that no one has experience in this matter. It will undoubtedly take all of us to cope with Joy's uniqueness—and steer her in appropriate directions."

"We acknowledge that, as Fourth Generation beings, the three of you may have insights which we cannot share," admitted Steele. "We are fine with that but ask that you keep us in the loop."

"Of course!" Andrea affirmed. "Leilani and I are quite aware of the challenge WE presented to our parents. We can only guess at the stress Joy is putting on hers—and on you!"

Nodding, the Nannies seemed to visibly relax. Then they looked over at the crib. Joy was standing! and laughing!

"How can she be standing?" cried Leilani. "She's only a couple of weeks old!" Startled, she suddenly found her arms full of a wiggling little babe, who was lifting her arms for a hug.

"One more thing," said Steele. "We have found that diapers are no longer necessary. Yesterday, she discovered the potty chair and is proud of using it!"

Mouths agape, the twins shook their heads in wonder. "Well, she certainly outdistanced us with that skill!" sighed Andrea. "We didn't achieve it for several months!"

"Is anything happening to that crystal on her tummy?" asked Leilani. "Also, Mama wants to know when her curls start changing color."

Marigold and Steele looked at each other. "Now that she is past the diaper stage, we won't be able to tell if there are changes in that crystal," commented Marigold. "As for her hair, it already changes—but we don't know why."

Crystos stared at Joy, who waved at him. When Leilani cuddled her, she smiled broadly, and her curls became pink. "We need to report this to the Queen immediately," he stressed. "With her life experience, she will be able to tell us what the colors mean."

The twins offered to tell their mother and handed Joy over to Marigold. Then they winked out of sight.

*   *   *   *   *

They found Tamara meditating in the Chapel. After exchanging hugs, they excitedly let her know about Joy's use of the potty chair, learning to stand in her crib—and the pink color of her curls when cuddled. Tamara sighed and said, "So it's begun. I'm not surprised about the developmental progress, but, for me, I had to reach puberty before these changes in color began to activate. I think our family is in for quite a ride!

"I had just finished making a list of colors and what they represented in my life. Joy may exhibit different colors, but perhaps my list will be useful. Please share it with Crystos and the Nannies. I'll give a copy to Candace," she promised.

"Candace and her siblings have had a good deal of experience with additional crystals appearing on their bodies when needed," she continued. "We'll have to be alert to similar occurrences happening to Joy."

"Mama," Andrea wondered, "Why haven't we had any crystals?"

"You do," Tamara stressed. "Your bracelets are crystal, and they enable you to conduct astral journeys."

"That's right," affirmed Leilani. "And who knows when others might appear. Plus, we are continually experiencing abilities that are Fourth Generation—which we then need to learn how to operate."

Accepting the list from her mother, Leilani grabbed Andrea's hand and they vanished. Tamara moved to a nearby couch and reflected on how important Solange and Savea had been to her in learning about her crystals. She hoped she would be as effective with her new sweet granddaughter. Meanwhile, she had to reach out to Sean and inform him about these new developments.

*   *   *   *   *

When Tamara suddenly appeared in his office, Sean knew something had happened. Putting his arm around her shoulder, he teleported into the Palace garden. A wave of his hand produced two glasses of wine and he led her to a vacant bench. "What's new, my love?" he asked, after kissing her deeply.

Chapter 6
Helping Joy

Tamara felt the need to talk directly to Solange and Savea. She sent them a mental summons to meet her in the Palace Chapel. While she waited, she sought solace in meditation.

A double flash of light announced their arrival. After exchanging hugs, Tamara invited them to sit beside her on the couch. She opened her mind to them and shared the recent progress of her granddaughter. Then she raised the basic question: "How can I help Joy the way you helped me? I had reached puberty; she is but a babe."

Solange and Savea grasped Tamara's hands and closed their eyes. Tamara could feel a surge of power flow through her…a feeling unlike any she had ever experienced. "What just happened?" she asked.

"We have shared with you everything we know about working with crystals," explained Solange. "After we helped you, we studied all available intel on that subject. We sensed that we would be called upon sometime in the future to revisit that knowledge. Apparently, that time is now."

"Tamara," pressed Savea, "would you please ask Candace to bring Joy here? We really haven't had a chance to know her."

"Of course," responded Tamara. "I should have thought of doing so." She closed her eyes and contacted her daughter. Within a few minutes, Marigold appeared with Joy sitting in a stroller (provided by Shamous, of course!).

Marigold explained that Candace was in Alteria, finalizing plans with Merlynn for the opening of the second play. "She had passed on your message and instructed me to comply—so here we are!"

Joy was bubbling with excitement and bouncing up and down. Her curls were yellow—apparently the color of that emotion.

Solange and Savea exchanged glances and knelt to hold Joy's hands. Joy closed her eyes and her hair returned to its normal white hue. "As we did with you, Tamara," reminded Savea, "we advised Joy that our goal was to help her keep her hair white...and she immediately made that happen! She's very advanced already."

"I know she's just a babe," Solange pondered, "but she seems to understand what we expect of her. I don't think you'll have any trouble training her—especially since you have personally experienced that training yourself."

Hugging Tamara, the Super Sisters promised to return

anytime to help Tamara with Joy's training. And they winked out of sight.

"Would you like Steele and me to work with you on this project with Joy?" asked Marigold.

"I would very much appreciate it," sighed Tamara. "Right now, I'm feeling overwhelmed—and bombarded with memories related to my own training. The Sisters focused on my learning to keep my hair white; but they also taught me the basics of my magic, like moving objects and lighting candles. When I arrived here in Marinea, I was totally clueless."

"Your Majesty," interrupted Marigold, "Look at Joy!"

Tamara dropped her gaze to the stroller and watched Joy waving her hands. The candles in the Chapel were flying around the room; some were lighted, and others were not. Then the lighted candles were extinguished, and the flames moved over to the non-lighted ones. Clearly, Joy had been listening to Tamara's comments about her personal training.

Grabbing a hymn book, Tamara placed it on the stroller's tray. She asked Joy to put it on the altar. Joy waved her hands and the book sailed through the air, landing gently on the altar.

She was so focused on Joy that she didn't hear Crystos enter the Chapel. When he began to clap, she flushed and explained that she was helping Joy with her powers. He nodded his approval and offered to join in that endeavor.

Marigold let him know that she and Steele would also be on the 'Joy Team.' He smiled and welcomed them aboard. Joy would have no lack of support!

*   *   *   *   *

Later that evening, when Marigold and Steele were getting Joy ready for bed, they watched a book sail across the Classroom. As it landed on the rocking chair, Steele picked it up and sat down. Suddenly, Joy was on his lap, looking up expectantly. Marigold laughed, "She wants you to read to her!"

Steele looked at Joy and asked, "Is that right? Should I read to you?"

Joy nodded and snuggled close to him. He noticed that it was a book of bedtime stories and began to read out loud. As he did so, Joy's eyes became heavy and started to close. When it was obvious that she had fallen asleep, he put down the book and carried her over to her crib. Tucking her in, he kissed her brow and tiptoed toward the door. Marigold dimmed the lights and they left the room.

"She's such a dear little girl," cooed Marigold. "I wonder how powerful she will be?"

Steele answered, "I have a feeling that she will teach us more than we will teach her. She's unique already."

In the crib, Joy smiled.

Chapter 7
Opening Night

The level of excitement in the Alteria Playhouse was palpable. The audience could feel it, even touch it. What would be called 'The Royal Box' in another kingdom was filled with the Elders who ruled Alteria, and their guests.

As the lights dimmed, a spotlight focused on a podium located Stage Right. Sunny walked in from the wings and took her place at the podium. After acknowledging the round of applause that welcomed her entrance, she began to present the rationale for the play that was about to begin.

Like her sister in the first play, Sunny's voice was clear and well-articulated. She allowed emotion to color her words, which set the tone for the events about to unfold in Act 1.

Candace stood in the wings and clapped furiously as Sunny left the stage, beginning Act 1. "You were wonderful, Sis," Candace enthused. "I just know this play will be a rousing success!"

Giving her sister a hug, Sunny returned to her dressing room. She wanted to prepare for her introduction to Act 2. She, also, had high hopes for how this second play would be received.

The play would run for one month in Alteria before the Touring Companies would be allowed to open in their various locations across Akura. This was by design. Merlynn and the Touring Directors had made a conscious decision to let the Touring Companies build upon the anticipated success of the Repertory Company, whose cast members welcomed the pressure.

Most of them had performed in the first play and fully expected this second play to be equally popular—if not even more. The theme of the second play was broader than that of the first, which was basically a documentary presentation of the history of the kingdom of Freedom. Play #2 portrayed values that spanned the globe.

*   *   *   *   *

At intermission, the audience gathered in the lobby to sample the bar service. The level of conversation was high. Merlynn strolled through the throng, trying to get a sense of the audience response. She had enlisted Leilani and Andrea to do the same; their heightened hearing would provide additional intel.

When the intermission had ended and the audience was filing back into the theater, she motioned to the twins to follow her and they walked into a private area. They shared what they had heard, and Merlynn was very pleased.

A bell sounded, indicating that Act 2 was about to begin, and the doors would be closed. Merlynn escorted the twins into the auditorium, and they took their seats.

*   *   *   *   *

When Sunny took her place at the podium to introduce Act 2, the applause was thunderous. She began by narrating a bridge between Acts 1 and 2. The audience gave her the gift of rapt attention and another ovation after her presentation.

Act 2 followed her narration seamlessly and, before long, it was time for a second intermission. The volume of the conversation was even louder than after Act 1. Merlynn found herself with a smile that kept growing broader. She could hardly wait to read the reviews!

When Sunny took the stage to introduce Act 3, the applause was overwhelming! There was a moment of silence before the curtain opened for Act 3.

As the curtain closed on Act 3 and the play ended, there was another moment of silence before the audience erupted with a standing ovation and cheers. The curtain opened for the last time, allowing the actors to take their bows. Then Merlynn took the stage to accept a bouquet of flowers and beckoned to the backstage crew to join her. More applause and sounds of appreciation erupted. The play was definitely a success. Now for the reviews…

*   *   *   *   *

The cast party was a mixture of celebration and nerves. What would the reviewers think? So much depended on their opinions. The hilarity of the party dropped as Merlynn entered with an armful of reviews.

Before she passed them around, she cautioned them by saying, "The reviews are mixed. This is not unexpected. Our play shone a light on pre-conceived prejudices and beliefs. The publications that addressed magical audiences were very enthusiastic; those that catered to non-magical ones were less so.

"Our play has a mission—to address fears and, hopefully, encourage openness. I urge you to take the positive reviews as an incentive to do even better—and negative reviews as a challenge. The 'New Friends' project that was the foundation of our play continues to prosper. Our play will prosper, too."

Then she distributed the reviews.

*   *   *   *   *

Merlynn stayed at the party until the last cast member had gone home, leaving her to do a needed post-mortem with her staff. They analyzed the reviews into the wee hours, fully supporting her comments to the cast.

Sunny pointed out that the true reviews had not as yet been received: future ticket sales. The first play had been slow to accumulate sales, but the end result was spectacular. She fully expected that this play would do equally as well. She urged everyone to be patient.

Skye asked Sunan to meet him for lunch the next day; they had some strategizing to do. He intended to invite Rose, as well.

Chapter 8
Improving the Play

"Lunch should be an interesting time," thought Skye as he prepared to meet his colleagues at the cafe. As he sat at the outdoor table that he had secured, he spied Sunan and Rose approaching from different directions.

Standing, he welcomed them, and they all took their seats. "Thank you for the luncheon invitation," said Sunan. Rose added her agreement. "Is this personal, or do you have an agenda?" continued Sunan.

"I'm hoping we can do both," replied Skye. "Have you had an opportunity to read the reviews of our opening night?"

Both Sunan and Rose nodded; their faces expressed some discontent. "I wish they had been more favorable," admitted Sunan. "But I understand the mental conflicts that inspired them."

Rose shook her head, "I am very familiar with the 'mental conflicts' you are referencing. I prefer to label them 'prejudices' and 'biases'. I encountered them frequently during the process of establishing the 'New Friends' projects. I believe that the underlying emotion is actually fear—fear of what is different, unfamiliar, and ultimately threatening to an established world view."

"And there you have it," summarized Skye. "You have articulated the basic challenge that we face—and must conquer."

"So how do you suggest that we approach this problem—so that our play can survive?" asked Sunan.

"While I don't have a ready answer to that question," admitted Skye, "I do know that the first step to solving a problem is identifying it—and I think we've just done that!"

*   *   *   *   *

The luncheon conversation continued through ordering, eating, and a lot of drinking. While no decision had been reached, Skye felt that great progress had been made in terms of exploring the parameters of the issues. Now they faced the hard part: designing strategies intended to change minds. They had reached consensus on one thing: they needed to invite Candace and the twins to their next meeting.

*   *   *   *   *

As Producer, Skye had automatically assumed the Chair role for the second meeting. However, instead of an outside table, he had elected to choose an inside one in a more private setting. As everyone settled into their chairs, he suggested that they order and enjoy lunch before addressing the substance of their meeting.

Having followed his lead, the luncheon participants had a pleasant lunch and were now ready to proceed with today's agenda. Present were Skye, as Chair, plus Sunan, Rose, Candace and the twins. When Skye began the meeting, he explained that everyone at the table had contributions to make—especially the three writers of the play's script.

The discussion proceeded across several hours, with the result that there would be some modifications to the script—with particular attention to the Narration. Everyone agreed that it was the Narration that offered the greatest possibility of changing minds. Therefore, Sunny should be invited to meeting #3.

Another approach engendering significant support was the creation of a more extensive playbill—one that would include data points reinforcing positive concepts for inclusion. One suggestion that proved popular was to present that data in an attractive cartoon format, or perhaps as a game. The twins offered to work with the playbill redesign—and they knew some students who would love to join them.

*   *   *   *   *

At the third meeting, it was clear that progress had been made. A revised Narration had been sent to Sunny for her review. The twins distributed copies of a proposed new playbill. When they had finished lunch, they were eager to discuss the proposed changes.

Sunny began by complimenting Candace and the twins on their alterations to the Narration script. She felt that significant new improvements had been made, both to her role and to the overall play script.

Then the conversation shifted to the playbill. The twins and their student friends had created an attractive document that would appeal to a variety of personal tastes—without being offensive.

When discussion had ended, a vote was taken and the revisions would be implemented with the next performance of the Repertory Play in Alteria. In addition, revised scripts would be sent to all Touring Companies around the planet.

Skye thanked everyone for their hard work and ordered a round of celebratory drinks for all.

*   *   *   *   *

Returning to the Pro Bono shop, Skye was delighted to find that Greta had returned from Starlight. Sharing a hug, they agreed to meet for dinner that evening.

Chapter 9
Dinner

Skye arrived at Greta's apartment, bearing an armful of flowers. She blushed, thanking him profusely, and went to get a vase of water. When she returned, they shared putting the blooms in the vase. Greta took one lovely blossom and put it behind her ear.

Gazing at her, Skye pulled Greta into a hug and kissed her deeply. Then, arm-in-arm, they left to walk to their favorite cafe. Skye had prearranged a reservation for a secluded table and was pleased with the one selected by the cafe management.

Once they had been comfortably seated, Skye created a cone of silence around them so that their privacy was secured. Only the server would be allowed to approach the table—as one was doing now, bearing some glasses and a bottle of sparkling wine.

Once their glasses were filled, they lifted them in a toast celebrating Greta's safe return from Starlight. They spent the next hour or so sharing what had transpired in their lives during their time apart. As they held hands across the table, they felt an unexpected flow of power between them. "Did you sense that?" asked Skye.

"Yes," answered Greta, "but what does it mean?"

"I'm not sure," admitted Skye, "but I wonder if it has something to do with the fact that you are a Super Twin—and I am not."

"I never thought about that," mused Greta, "but you are right. We are different in that respect. You and your siblings are unique in the universe."

At that moment, Terra joined their table.

"You have discovered an important attribute, Skye. You and your three siblings are inter-related in a very special way. While not having Super Twins, you have each other and your combined powers will prove to be very significant," she said. "There will come a time in your lives when those joint powers will be critical, and your spouses will be important assets." Then she vanished.

Skye and Greta looked at each other in stunned silence. "What did she mean?" asked Greta in a voice that trembled.

"I have no idea," admitted Skye. "But I certainly intend to try and find out. Meanwhile, let's not let this uncertainty ruin our dinner." As if on cue, the server reappeared to take their order.

As they awaited their dinner, Greta excused herself. While she was gone, Skye sent a mental message to his parents and three siblings, asking for a meeting at breakfast in the Private Dining Room tomorrow. Then his full attention returned to Greta as she rejoined him.

The rest of the evening went smoothly and the server once again appeared—with a special dessert offering: a luscious cake to be shared. Nestled into the frosting was a small box made of chocolate. As the server cut slices of cake and presented them to his two diners, he also took a spoon and lifted the chocolate box—placing it on top of Greta's slice.

With a puzzled look, Greta picked up the chocolate box and opened it. Gasping, she removed a magnificent ring. As she did so, Skye knelt before her and took her hand. Gazing into her eyes, he asked her to share his life path. As she nodded, he placed the ring on her finger and, even though the other patrons couldn't hear him, they still stood and clapped!

With a wave, Skye caused the cone of silence to become opaque, securing their privacy. He put his arms around Greta and kissed her deeply, completing the design he had created for the evening.

Murmuring words of love, he added the hope that Terra's prophecy had not tarnished the evening. Greta sighed and assured him that, together, they could face whatever the future held for them.

*   *   *   *   *

At breakfast the next morning, Skye related the events of the previous evening. Everyone clapped at the news of his betrothal. He accepted their good wishes with a smile—and then reported Terra's visit and message.

Stunned, the four siblings looked at their parents with worry on their faces. Sean put his arm around Tamara's shoulders as she began to tremble. "I'm sorry, children," she began. "I don't have any intel to share with you. I'm sure that Mother had her reasons for interrupting your festive dinner. But at this time, I don't have any explanation for you. When I do, I'll share it with you immediately."

Sean added, "I have to interpret her words as a warning that we will be facing some event or events that will test our resolve. I advise you to be alert and report anything that you find to be unusual or unexpected. Meanwhile, Skye, don't be dismayed. Your future has just been made more meaningful— enjoy the ride!"

Everyone clapped and congratulated Skye again. Assurances of love and support made him feel much better. However, his senses were now activated at a higher level. He had to be ready for whatever was to come.

Chapter 10
Wedding Bells are Ringing

Skye was troubled by Terra's words, but he recognized that he couldn't let himself be distracted; he needed to focus on the reality of his successful proposal to Greta. Now that she was back from Starlight, they fell into the natural rhythm they had established in the operation of the Pro Bono shop.

That rhythm prevented sharing a lunch date, since they preferred that one of them would be present in the shop at all times. However, since they closed the shop for the day at dinnertime, they began a new tradition of a daily dinner date.

That evening, after taking their seats at their favorite cafe, they both began to speak at the same time—asking the same question: "Shall we set a date for our wedding?"

Laughing, Skye leaned in to give his now-fiancée a kiss. "We seem to be thinking alike," he commented. "Since it seems to be top-of-mind for both of us, let's talk about it."

Greta nodded and asked, "Do you prefer a long or short engagement?"

"Personally," Skye began, "I'd like to wed you tomorrow!"

Giggling, Greta agreed, "I feel the same way. So let's keep that feeling in mind as we chat." A flash of light announced the arrival of Shamous at their table. Stunned, Skye and Greta stammered some words of welcome.

"I hope I didn't startle you too much," apologized Shamous, "but I sensed that you were about to make some important decisions—and I would like to offer my services."

Skye and Greta shared a glance and Skye shook Shamous' hand. "With your track record," Skye began, "how could we refuse?"

"But we have just begun the wedding conversation," Greta pointed out. "No decisions have been made so far."

"On the contrary," insisted Shamous, "you have already made the most important one: you wish to wed as soon as possible. Am I not correct?"

Flushing, Skye and Greta had to admit that Shamous was right, but they had no idea how to make their wish a reality. "That's where I come in," said Shamous.

A server appeared to take their order. Shamous took him aside and requested a celebratory bottle of wine. Smiling, the server left and the wedding conversation continued.

Having become somewhat of an expert on wedding planning recently, Shamous could easily steer the conversation into the decision-making lane. He knew what questions to ask in order to arrive at the necessary decision points.

Some important intel soon emerged: a deep love of the law and justice for all, as demonstrated by the successful Pro Bono shop; a preference for classical music, particularly opera; and a shared appreciation for flowers and greenery.

After dinner had been enjoyed, Shamous waved his hand and produced a list of ideas for the wedding:

- Venue: the Marinean Courthouse, which had a large reception hall for the reception.

- Music: from their favorite opera, presented by the local opera company and a small orchestra situated in the courtroom balcony.

- Decor: a flower garden.

- Bridal party: soft green, with witnesses in flowery colors.

- Officiant: the Head Judge of the kingdom.

Skye and Greta stared at Shamous and then at each other. "How does he do it?" asked Greta.

Skye shook his head in bewilderment, "I have no idea, but he seems to get it right every time!"

"The Courthouse is available in one moon's time," informed Shamous. "Will that be acceptable?"

As Skye and Greta nodded helplessly, Shamous reached behind him and set a box on the table. Looking inside, Greta exclaimed, "These are wedding invitations! How…?"

Shamous smiled, "I have my ways, my dear."

"We need to let the Palace know as soon as possible," insisted Skye. "Greta, I just realized that I don't know anything about your family…"

"I never mentioned them because I was an orphan, Skye," she admitted. "In fact, I have no childhood memories at all—until I was nearly grown."

Skye was astonished! Of course! She was a Super Child and a late bloomer. "Well, you'll have a family now, Sweetheart," he said as he hugged her to him.

"One more thing," added Shamous. "Skye, I fully understand that your mother needs to have a role in this planning. I shall make that happen." And he vanished.

Calling the server over, Skye ordered another bottle of wine!

Chapter 11
"All Rise!"

It was the day of the wedding of Skye and Greta. True to his promise, Shamous had found a host of opportunities for Tamara to be involved. She knew what he was doing—but she was very grateful!

When she arrived at the Courthouse, she was escorted to a room where members of the bridal party would be gathered. She knew that her ultimate destination was the Jury Box within the Courtroom.

Across the hall, another room was designated for the witnesses: Verd and Steele for the Groom; Moonstone and Trixie for the Bride. Skye had asked to be included in this group, as his bridal attire was not a secret like the Bride's gown. He wore a formal suit in a moss green hue, as did his witnesses. However, his witnesses also sported an ascot in a flowery design. That design was repeated in the gowns worn by the Bride's witnesses. As they walked into the Courtroom, they would look like a garden in motion.

At an undisclosed location within the Courthouse, Greta was being assisted by Candace, Sunny, Leilani and Andrea—

her new Sisters-in-law. As she donned her gown, a sudden reality hit her: she had a family at last... and tears appeared in her eyes.

Leilani offered her a tissue and hugged her briefly. "You look so beautiful, Greta," Leilani praised, a sentiment echoed by the other girls. Greta twirled, her gown swirling around her: a moss green overskirt with flowered underskirts beneath. Once again, Shamous had delivered the perfect bridal attire.

A flash of light and Moonstone appeared, prepared to escort her Super Twin to the Courtroom. They embraced with emotion, as the other girls teleported to the bridal party room. It was time for the ceremony to begin.

Tamara led the occupants of the bridal party room into the Courtroom and over to the Jury Box. Sean remained at the door; he would be the official escort of Greta down the aisle.

As he waited, the witnesses teleported to the door and began to enter the Courtroom. Last in the procession was Moonstone, who preceded the Bride. Greta took Sean's arm and they began their movement down the aisle.

Skye gazed lovingly at his Bride, who blushed at his attention. Sean placed Greta's hand into Sean's and took his place in the Jury Box. Candace accepted the bridal bouquet as the Bailiff intoned, "All rise!" The Judge entered the Courtroom, and he greeted the Bride and Groom.

The Judge's opening remarks focused on the contributions the Pro Bono shop had given to the community. He emphasized that it was his honor to officiate over this ceremony.

Music from the balcony set the stage and the wedding service began.

*   *   *   *   *

It was late in the day and the reception was in full swing. Wine flowed freely and couples twirled around the dance floor installed in the Courthouse reception area. Skye and Greta took full advantage of the orchestra and their favorite dance tunes. Greta whispered in his ear, "After I throw the bouquet, where will we go? I don't remember planning anything."

Skye looked confused and then admitted that he had no memory of that either. Just then, Shamous tapped him on the shoulder. "I think it's time for the bouquet toss," he said, handing Greta her bouquet.

Greta took the flowers and climbed up on a chair. Turning her back, she tossed the blooms into the air, where—like previous weddings—they hung in the air as if looking around the room. Finding their target, they fell into the arms of…Andrea!

Tamara gasped, thinking "NO, she's too young!" Turning to Sean, she looked into his eyes with a sense of panic.

Sean held her close, trying to allay her fears. "Some of these wedding bouquets seem to be expressing a kind of celestial prophecy," he proposed. "So far, their selections have proved to be good choices, don't you agree?"

Tamara nodded, but there were tears in her eyes. "Has Andrea been seeing someone without telling us?" she asked.

"Only one person comes to mind," replied Sean. "Skye told me that she and Stefan seemed close. I'll keep an eye on him now that he will be continuing his studies here in Marinea. Don't worry, my dear."

Tamara sighed in resignation. "This is a totally unexpected development," she complained. "I hope the universe isn't making a mistake this time."

*　　*　　*　　*　　*

Meanwhile, Shamous was once again approaching the newlyweds. "I heard you commenting that you don't remember planning anything after the reception. There's a reason for that: it's a surprise!"

Skye and Greta looked at him with a sense of bewilderment on their faces. Shamous continued, "I knew you would be unwilling to both be absent from the Pro Bono shop, so I 'mentioned' it to the Judge—and he has offered to manage it while you have a few weeks to yourselves. Just tell me where you would like to go, and I will make it happen."

Stars in their eyes, they whispered a desired location in his ear—and it was done.

The Judge stood and made an official announcement that he would be in charge of the Pro Bono shop while they were away…and the wedding guests gave him a thunderous ovation!

Chapter 12
A Clear and Future Danger

After Tamara and Sean returned to the Palace after the wedding, they began to prepare for bed. However, Tamara was on edge and restless. Sean tried to comfort her, casting a soothing spell.

"I love weddings, Sean. I really do," she protested. "And I did take note that all FOUR of our first-born children are now happily wed. But, somehow, I just can't wrap my mind around the possibility that our darling Andrea has been targeted! And WHY? By some celestial puppeteer?"

"Take a deep breath, Sweetheart," he advised. "The only puppeteer that I can think of is…"

"The Creator Being!" she cried, completing his sentence. "MOTHER!" she yelled.

A flash of light and Terra joined them, seated on a nearby couch. "I was waiting for your summons, Tamara. When I saw that bouquet drop, I knew you would be upset."

"Is this another of the Creator Being's plots?" asked Tamara testily. "Andrea isn't old enough to be contemplating a life path change. She's still in school!"

"I don't know for certain," replied Terra, "but my instincts tell me that your assumption may be true."

"But what could the endgame be?" Tamara wondered aloud.

"I'm sorry, but I don't have any answers for you," apologized Terra. "I'm aware that your number FOUR has surfaced again with the wedding of your fourth first-born. Do you have any other combinations in mind where that number might have a role?"

"Right now, I can't think of any," Tamara responded, "but I'm certainly going to raise my awareness."

"If anything occurs to you, please let me know—and I'll do the same," promised Terra as she vanished.

Sean picked Tamara up and carried her to the bed, tucking her in lovingly. Kissing her gently, he waved his hand to dim the lights.

*   *   *   *   *

Tamara was tossing and turning in bed, moaning as she did so. Awakened, Sean held her closely and tried to calm her. "I'm so frightened, Sean," she sobbed. "Something terrible is going to happen, but I don't know what!"

"Would you like me to call Crystos?" he inquired. "Sometimes he has access to the future."

"YES!" Tamara cried out. "Anything to shed some light on what is coming!"

Sean sent a mental message to Crystos, asking him to meet in the Chapel. He and Tamara dressed and walked over to the Chapel, finding that Crystos was already waiting for them.

"It's the middle of the night," observed Crystos. "Is something wrong?"

Tamara shared her stress and fears with him, hoping that he might have some insight into their cause. Crystos closed his eyes, breathing deeply. Finally, he spoke, "This is not your imagination, Your Majesty. You are sensing something dark that is approaching. I'm sorry that I can't be more specific, but I can tell you that we are about to face a significant danger and had best be very aware."

Tamara began to tremble uncontrollably. Sean put his arms around her and promised to establish defensive perimeters everywhere until the danger presented itself. Crystos bowed and took his leave, listening to Temara sobbing behind him.

*   *   *   *   *

After a night of disturbed sleep, Tamara awoke feeling anxious and distressed. Sean tried to allay her fears, but was unsuccessful. Finally, he decided to summon Terra in the hope that she might be able to help.

As always, Terra arrived promptly and led her daughter to a nearby couch. Puttiing her arm around Tamara's shoulders, Terra asked, "What is troubling you, my dear?"

Tears streamed down Tamara's cheeks as she confessed her apprehension about the danger that was hovering over her kingdom. She reported the warning that Crystos had shared and, once again, started sobbing. "I feel so helpless, Mother. Obviously, there is great danger coming and I don't know what to do."

Terra admitted that she had become aware of an impending crisis, but added that the Creator Being was being mostly silent. All she was told was, "Look up."

"Look up?" cried Tamara. "What does that mean?"

"I don't know yet, dear," said Terra. "But if I hear anything more, I'll let you know. In the meantime, try and raise your spirits. You have a kingdom to rule." Giving her daughter a kiss on the cheek, she disappeared.

Tamara sighed and began to dress for the day.

*   *   *   *   *

As was her practice, Tamara often held open audiences so that citizens could present their concerns. Today was one of those days. When the doors to the Throne Room opened, she was startled to see a familiar group at the head of the line waiting to talk to her: the most esteemed astronomers in the kingdom. She gestured for them to approach. Recognizing the woman who stepped forward, she invited her to present their petition.

"Your Majesty, we bring news that is of great import. As you know, we use telescopes to monitor the skies and the stars. Normally, we can do so easily—and we have done so for many millennia. However, just recently, the skies have gone dark; we no longer can observe the stars."

Chapter 13
The Darkness

Tamara gasped, "How recently?"

When the answer was given, Tamara realized that the darkness had first been noticed just after she and the others had returned from the astral journey assessing the potential planets for the relocation of the inhabitants of Planet X.

"Is it possible that a Super Nova could cause this mysterious darkness?" she asked, fearfully.

The astronomers turned and conferred among themselves. "We have never observed one, Your Majesty, but—theoretically—it could be possible. A Super Nova would destroy all nearby planets, potentially creating a multitude of asteroids, sending them into the universe. Such a catastrophe has undoubtedly happened before, since asteroids are part of the cosmic landscape."

"Would such an occurrence block the light of stars that are further away, preventing you from observing them for a period of time?" pressed Tamara.

"We believe so, Your Majesty. You are asking questions

that suggest prior knowledge of such a potential celestial event. Could you elaborate?"

Tamara found herself clutching the arms of her throne so tightly that her hands were turning white. Up to this point, she had kept her ability to conduct astral journeys a state secret. Clearly, that would no longer be either possible or desirable. She sent a mental summons to Sean to join her in the Throne Room—and to bring his memory wipe gadget.

When he arrived, she opened her mind to him so that he understood what had just occurred. She asked him to escort the group of astronomers to a nearby conference room. She would join them as soon as the open audience ended.

*   *   *   *   *

Fortunately, she was able to conclude the audience rather rapidly, as not too many petitioners remained. When she arrived at the conference room, she discovered that Sean had been thoroughly briefed by the group of astronomers about Super Novas and their consequences.

As Sean pulled out a chair for her, he whispered a question, "Are you going to go public with your astral journey ability?"

Nodding, she began to describe in detail what her crystal bracelets allowed her to do—and the results of the most recent astral journey. She emphasized that the intel she was sharing

58

was classified—and on a 'need-to- know' basis, which did not include the general public.

"The good news is that we were able to identify a suitable planet for the Planet X population. That relocation has been completed successfully. The bad news, apparently, is that the star Planet X orbited around has apparently turned into a Super Nova," she explained. "Now we must deal with the consequences."

*   *   *   *   *

The meeting with the astronomers had turned into a gaggle of excitable voices and proposed theories. She locked eyes with Sean and then asked the female astronomer who had originally brought the issue to her attention to step outside the room with her. Nodding at Sean, she authorized him to use his device.

She escorted the astronomer to her office and invited her to sit in the chair opposite the desk. "You appear to have the clearest head in that group. How do you feel about the intel I shared?"

"Your Majesty, I'm obviously worried about how our kingdom will be affected by this cosmic event. But I'm afraid that what I just experienced in that conference room will promote panic in the population."

"Then we agree," approved Tamara. "I would like to appoint you as a Special Scientific Consultant to the Crown, if you are willing to accept that responsibility. I am aware of your significant background, Dr. Hanover."

"I would be honored, Your Majesty," replied Dr. Hanover. "But what about my colleagues?"

"Commander Sean will see to them," promised Tamara. "As we speak, he is wiping their memory of this meeting. It will be one of your first challenges to propose a competing theory about the darkness that will satisfy them. You may share the intel about your new role in the Palace—as long as you do not divulge relevant details. I hope you're a good actress!"

Blushing, Dr. Hanover said, "I'll do my best, Your Majesty. Right now, I don't see a path forward to handle the threat of multiple asteroid strikes. Do you?"

"I have some ideas," admitted Tamara. "I am going to ask my four first-born children to meet me tomorrow for lunch here in the Palace. I would like you to attend that meeting."

"Of course," agreed Dr. Hanover.

"Please bring any data that you have concerning Super Novas and asteroids. I'm sure we're going to need it."

As Dr. Hanover stood to leave the office, she didn't notice that Tamara cast a spell once her back was turned.

About the Author

After doing academic writing during my 20 years as Professor at the University of Wisconsin-Madison, I retired to Hawai'i in 1999. A decade later, I began being aware of an interesting fantasy story line in my mind and began writing it soon after. It was an occasional hobby for another decade and then the book became impatient with me and began to seriously nudge me. Since I began "listening" to the book, the writing has been a fun and all-encompassing part of my life.

I have completed 12 books in my Crystal Saga Series 1 and 12 books in Crystal Saga Series 2. I have completed books 1 through 8 in my Crystal Saga Series 3 and I am now working on books 9 and 10. Stay tuned for more.

Crystal Saga Series 1 by
D. E. Weingand

Scan the QR Code with Your Cell Phone to Order Books. Or go to LuLu.com, Amazon.com, Barnsandnoble.com and many other outlets.

Crystal Saga Series 2 by
D. E. Weingand

Book 1 — Exploration

Book 2 — More Mysteries

Book 3 — Escalation

Book 4 — Renewals

Book 5 — New Beginnings

Book 6 — More Crystals

Book 7 — The World Changes

Book 8 — Romance Blossoms

Book 9 — New (Ad)Ventures

Book 10 — (Ad)Ventures Continue

Book 11 — Designing the Future

Book 12 — The Future Beckons

Crystal Saga Series 3 by
D. E. Weingand

Book 1 — The Next Generations

Book 2 — Into the Future

Book 3 — The Fourth Generation

Book 4 — Starlight

Book 5 — Exploring Starlight

Book 6 — The Planet of Starlight

Book 7 — The Saga of Planet X . . . and Beyond

Book 8 — What's Next?

Coming Soon

Book 9 — Dealing with Darkness

Book 10 — TBA